Lorelei Dro
Bouquet As Everything Went Dark.

Jack tossed the sheet over her head and then she felt herself being lifted from the floor and flung over a shoulder—a hard, muscular shoulder. And suddenly they were moving.

Just as the first notes of "The Wedding March" sounded, Lorelei felt the blast of July heat hit her and realized they had exited the church. She'd just been kidnapped from her wedding! This can't be happening, she thought. Shock turned to anger as she attempted to get free.

"Be still," Jack commanded, patting her on her rear.

"Jack! Take me back to my wedding!"

"Sorry, beautiful. That's something I'm not willing to do."

"Why not?" she demanded.

"Because, sweetheart, you promised a long time ago to marry me, and I've decided to hold you to that promise."

Dear Reader,

LET'S CELEBRATE FIFTEEN YEARS
OF SILHOUETTE DESIRE...

with some of your favorite authors and new stars of tomorrow. For the next three months, we present a spectacular lineup of unforgettably romantic love stories—led by three MAN OF THE MONTH titles.

In October, Diana Palmer returns to Desire with *The Patient Nurse,* which features an unforgettable hero. Next month, Ann Major continues her bestselling CHILDREN OF DESTINY series with *Nobody's Child.* And in December, Dixie Browning brings us her special brand of romantic charm in *Look What the Stork Brought.*

But Desire is not only MAN OF THE MONTH! It's new love stories from talented authors Christine Rimmer, Helen R. Myers, Raye Morgan, Metsy Hingle and new star Katherine Garbera in October.

In November, don't miss sensuous surprises from BJ James, Lass Small, Susan Crosby, Eileen Wilks and Shawna Delacorte.

And December will be filled with Christmas cheer from Maureen Child, Kathryn Jensen, Christine Pacheco, Anne Eames and Barbara McMahon.

Remember, here at Desire we've been committed to bringing you the very best in unforgettable romance and sizzling sensuality. And to add to the excitement of fifteen wonderful years, we offer the chance for you to win some wonderful prizes. Look in the pages at the end of the book for details.

And may we have many more years of happy reading together!

Melissa Senate

Senior Editor

Please address questions and book requests to:
Silhouette Reader Service
U.S.: 3010 Walden Ave., P.O. Box 1325, Buffalo, NY 14269
Canadian: P.O. Box 609, Fort Erie, Ont. L2A 5X3

METSY HINGLE

THE KIDNAPPED BRIDE

SILHOUETTE BOOKS

ISBN 0-373-76103-1

THE KIDNAPPED BRIDE

This edition published by arrangement with Harlequin Books S.A.

Printed in U.S.A.

Books by Metsy Hingle

Silhouette Desire

Seduced #900
Surrender #978
Backfire #1026
Lovechild #1055
**The Kidnapped Bride* #1103

*Right Bride, Wrong Groom

METSY HINGLE

is a native of New Orleans who loves the city in which she grew up. She credits the charm of her birthplace, and her own French heritage, with instilling in her the desire to write. Married and the mother of four children, she believes in romance and happy endings. Becoming a Silhouette author is a long-cherished dream come true for Metsy and one happy ending that she continues to celebrate with each new story she writes. She loves hearing from readers. Write to Metsy at P.O. Box 3224, Covington, LA 70433.

For Jean and Jeanne Wilson,
for all the years of friendship,
for all the years of love.

One

"You don't have to go through with it, you know. It's not too late to back out."

Lorelei Mason dragged her attention from the sight of her future mother-in-law being escorted down the aisle of the church and stared at her younger sister. Dressed in rose-colored silk that set off her creamy skin and the reddish gold of her hair, her sister Desiree looked at her out of troubled eyes. "It's not too late to back out of what?"

"The wedding," Desiree informed her, darting a quick glance at the church doors. "If you're having second thoughts about marrying Herbert, then you shouldn't do it. It's not too late to say you've changed your mind."

"What makes you think I'm having second thoughts?" Lorelei asked even as she felt the knot of apprehension tighten in her stomach again. She wasn't having second thoughts about marrying Herbert Van Owen III. She was having third, fourth and fifth thoughts about marrying him and had been for the past two weeks—ever since Jack

Storm had showed up in Mesa. The blasted man, Lorelei thought, frowning. She hadn't expected to ever see him again, nor had she wanted to. So what was a sea-loving pirate like him doing here in the Arizona desert? And why now, just when she was about to get married?

"Because you don't look the way a bride should look on her wedding day."

At her sister's remark, Lorelei shoved thoughts of Jack from her mind. She looked down at her white lace-and-satin wedding gown—the one she'd ordered months ago from the bridal store in Phoenix and had paid an outrageous two weeks' salary for. She made a point of checking her matching white shoes and the bouquet of ivory roses and lilies in her hand. Arching her brow, she leveled her younger sibling with the look of superiority and wisdom that her almost two years' advantage in age gave her. "That's funny. *I* think I look like a bride. And I know I'm certainly dressed for the part."

Desiree let out a dramatic sigh that bespoke her stage training. "You're always so literal, Lorelei," she said, making a face. "I wasn't talking about your dress. I was talking about *you*. *You* don't look the way a bride should look on her wedding day."

"And how is it I'm supposed to look?" Lorelei asked imperiously. She would not let her baby sister cause her to start second-guessing herself. Her decision to marry Herbert had been a sound one, made after carefully considering the pros and cons. Her stomach did another somersault, and Lorelei fought against the uneasy feeling. It's nerves, she told herself. She just needed to get this wedding over and done with. She cut a glance toward the vestibule. What in the world was keeping her father and older sister? How long did it take to adjust a cummerbund anyway?

"You should look…happy."

She shifted her attention back to her sister. "I *am* happy," Lorelei informed her.

"But you don't...glow. A bride should glow on her wedding day," Desiree said dreamily.

Lorelei blinked. Glow? She was expected to glow when she was having a hard time not losing the coffee and toast she'd managed to force down sometime before noon that day? "I'm not a light bulb, for pity's sake. And I don't know any women who walk around glowing on their wedding day or any other day." Except maybe her mother. There had always been a glow about her mother whenever she looked at Lorelei's father. "That's just another one of those foolish ideas the media uses to help sell a poor, prospective bride a lot of unnecessary products."

"No, it's not," Desiree insisted as she fidgeted with the sprig of pink and white roses in her bouquet.

Lorelei narrowed her eyes at the movement. What was wrong with her sister? Desiree *never* fidgeted. Or at least not since they'd been children. And then only when she'd done something she felt guilty about.

"The media has nothing to do with it. On her wedding day a bride should glow with happiness. And you don't."

All right. So she didn't glow, Lorelei conceded silently. There was no surprise in that since she didn't feel like a glowing bride, either. But then, she was almost twenty-nine now, not some starry-eyed teenager who believed in such romantic nonsense. She was a responsible and levelheaded woman. And she refused to let her sister's remark get to her. "Desiree, sweetie, you've obviously played one too many romantic leads."

"This has nothing to do with my acting."

"Then what *is* this all about? And for heaven sakes, stop that fidgeting. Why are you so nervous anyway? You're not the one getting married. I am."

"Oh, Lorelei." Desiree caught her hand and squeezed it.

Uneasiness climbed up Lorelei's spine again at her sister's solemn expression. "What? What's wrong?"

Desiree blinked back tears. "You're my sister and I love

you. I just don't want to see you make a mistake that you'll regret for the rest of your life."

Taken aback, Lorelei asked, "What makes you think I'll regret marrying Herbert?"

"Because I don't think you really love him. And if you don't love him, you shouldn't marry him."

"That's ridiculous," Lorelei told her, pulling her hand free. The knot tightened in her stomach again.

"No, it's not. I think you *want* to love Herbert. I really believe you do. But you can't because you're really still in love with Jack and—"

"Don't you dare mention that...that scoundrel's name to me," Lorelei ordered, unable to keep the heat out of her voice. Of all days, her wedding day was not when she wanted to be reminded of Jack Storm and what a fool she had been where he was concerned.

"But—"

"All set?" her father asked as he and her sister Clea joined them.

"Yes," Lorelei said, pulling herself together. She pinned Desiree with a look that said the discussion was closed.

"Then let's get this show on the road," Henry Mason told her.

"You okay?" Clea asked. "You look...upset."

"I'm fine. I just want to get this over with," she said, her voice clipped. At the slight lifting of Clea's dark brow, Lorelei softened her tone and said, "Sorry. Bridal jitters, I guess."

Clea smiled. "Which is another reason I'm glad it's you getting married and not me."

Lorelei forced a smile, then gave a nod to the organist to begin the processional. Music filled the church, and Lorelei's stomach took another nosedive as Clea moved to the center of the entranceway and prepared to walk down the aisle.

"My boutonniere," Henry Mason exclaimed. "I left it in the room."

"Daddy, don't worry about it. You don't need it."

"Nonsense. I can't walk my little girl down the aisle and not be properly dressed. Besides, your mother would never let me hear the end of it." Smiling, he patted her cheek. "I'll be right back."

Lorelei's palms grew damp as her older sister started down the aisle. The flowers in her hands started to shake, and Lorelei tightened her grip, strangling the stem of the bouquet. She felt hot. She felt cold. Her head started to buzz. She pressed her hand to her stomach, feeling as though a war had been launched inside it. Stop it, Lorelei commanded and attempted to regain control of herself.

It *was* bridal jitters, just as she had told Clea. All brides went through this. Of course she wanted to marry Herbert. She'd known him for four years, had been engaged to him for the past two.

I don't think you really love Herbert.

Desiree's words played over in her mind, but Lorelei shut them out. All right. So maybe there weren't any fireworks when Herbert kissed her, but that didn't mean she didn't love him. Of course she loved him. And she was going to marry him.

Clea reached the midway point, and Desiree stepped to the center of the doorway, preparing to precede Lorelei down the aisle to the altar, where Herbert waited.

Lorelei swallowed past a fresh bout of nerves as the music played on and the organist gave the cue for Desiree to begin going down the aisle.

Desiree hesitated in the doorway and turned to face her. There it was again, the guilt in her baby sister's eyes. "Lorelei, I'm sorry. I just want you to be happy. I hope you'll forgive me."

Confused, Lorelei stared at her sister. "Forgive you for what?"

"For stopping you from marrying the wrong man."

Lorelei whipped around at the sound of Jack's voice. She froze. For a moment she couldn't move. She couldn't speak. She simply stared at him. He stood there in the back of the church looking bigger than life in his faded jeans and denim shirt, his dark hair curling at his neck, his sinful blue eyes gleaming mischievously. She looked down at his hands, big and bronzed from the sun, and holding what appeared to be a sheet.

"Hello, beautiful," he said, flashing her a smile.

The familiar endearment snapped her from the spell. "What are you—?"

Jack tossed the sheet over her head, and Lorelei dropped her bouquet as everything went dark. She grabbed at the sheet, tried to push it away from her face.

"Aghhh," Lorelei attempted to scream, and managed to swallow a mouthful of cotton sheet. Then she felt herself being lifted from the floor and flung over a shoulder—a hard, muscular shoulder.

And then suddenly they were moving.

Just as the first notes of the wedding march sounded, Lorelei felt the blast of July heat hit her and realized they had exited the church. This can't be happening, she thought. It can't be. Shock turned to anger, and she renewed her attempts to get free.

"Be still," Jack commanded, smacking her on her rear.

Lorelei gasped and got another mouthful of sheet. Furious, she started to kick her legs, only to have her stomach, which had been churning all day, turn over at the bumpy trip down what was obviously the church steps.

It would serve him right if she got sick all over him. And she'd ruin her wedding dress. Her wedding! She'd just been kidnapped from her wedding. The strains of the church music grew more distant, and Lorelei kicked out again, only to earn another swat to her bottom. Outraged, she was just about to kick again when she felt herself being dumped into the seat of some type of vehicle and strapped in with what had to be a safety harness.

She heard the door slam next to her and another one open on the other side. When the engine started, she renewed her fight through the tangle of sheet and wedding veil. Finally she managed to get her head free. A thick section of fawn-colored hair fell across her right cheekbone and eye—a casualty of her upswept hairdo. Her carefully and expensively styled hairdo. Pushing it away from her face, she glared at Jack. "How dare you!"

He shifted the truck into reverse and executed a swift turn that sent her body sideways and did nothing to ease her stomach.

"What do you think you're doing?" she demanded, still fighting to get the rest of her body free from the imprisoning sheet.

"I told you," he said, giving her a wink and that devilish smile again. "I'm stopping you from marrying the wrong man." Then he shifted and sent the vehicle speeding past the church.

"You're crazy!"

"Probably."

Lorelei twisted in her seat, and another curl tumbled into her eyes. She shoved it away in time to see her sister Desiree standing on the church steps, a guilty expression written all over her face.

Jack made a sharp turn, and Lorelei's wedding veil plopped into her lap. She stared at the crushed tulle trimmed with tiny seed pearls and looked back at the church that was rapidly shrinking from view. What would her parents think? What would Herbert think?

Herbert! Oh, mercy, he and his mother were waiting for her at the church. She swallowed a groan as she thought of the formidable Mrs. Van Owen II and what she would say. The woman would never forgive her if she ruined Herbert's wedding. "Stop! I demand you stop this instant!"

Jack ignored her.

Lorelei yanked away the rest of the sheet and threw it on the floor. "Jack Storm, either you turn this thing around right now or I'll...I'll jump out."

"I wouldn't recommend doing that," he said calmly, pushing his foot down on the accelerator. "You'd end up splattering that pretty face of yours on the road, and I'd just come back and get you anyway."

Lorelei swallowed past the lump in her throat as she watched the speedometer climb to near eighty. She looked at the smug expression on his face. Refusing to let him intimidate her, she unhooked her seat belt and grabbed the handle of the door. "I mean it, Jack. Stop or I'll jump out."

He continued to ignore her. He didn't think she'd do it, she realized. He thought she didn't have the guts. Hadn't he accused her of as much two weeks ago when she'd refused to meet with him? She'd show him. How hard could it be? Stunt people did this all the time for a living. She'd seen them do it countless times on movie sets when she'd been growing up and shuffling from one location to another with her parents. One of the extras whose makeup her mother had done had even shown her how it was done. Tuck and roll. That's all she had to do. Tuck and roll. Taking a deep breath, Lorelei pushed down on the handle and shoved against the door.

Nothing happened.

She caught Jack's smirk. More determined than ever, she punched the unlock button and heard another click just as she jerked down on the door handle.

Jack moved his hand from the driver's-door panel back to the wheel. Flashing her another smile, he said, "These new automatic-lock features are pretty amazing. I'll have to remember to write the manufacturer and thank them for making it standard equipment."

Anger escalated to fury, and Lorelei clenched her hands into fists. She wanted to hit him. She wouldn't give him the satisfaction. She wasn't the same reckless girl she'd been ten years ago. She was older, wiser and not given to emotional outbursts. "Jack, I demand you take me back right now."

"Sorry, beautiful. Can't do that. If I took you back, you'd marry that stuffed shirt, Herbert."

"I *want* to marry Herbert. And he is not a stuffed shirt!"

Jack snorted and continued to cruise down the highway. "Sure, he is. Why else would the guy have been wearing a suit and tie in the middle of the week in this heat?" he asked, reminding her of their encounter two weeks ago.

"At least he owns a suit and tie," Lorelei countered.

Jack shrugged, obviously unfazed by the barb. "And the fellow's got sissy hands. I swear when he shook hands with me they were as soft as a baby's bottom. I bet he even has them manicured."

"I happen to like the way Herbert dresses and I like his hands."

"Hey, if it turns you on, I'll get a suit and tie," he said. "But that's where I draw the line. No way am I going to let anybody slap sweet-smelling creams on *my* hands."

Lorelei looked at Jack's hands gripping the steering wheel. Large and strong, with a long white scar that sliced through the bronzed skin on his right hand. There was nothing soft or nice about Jack Storm's hands. There never had been. His were a man's hands—roughened and callused by hard work and physical labor. Yet she knew just how gentle those hands could be. How carefully they could unearth a delicate seashell buried in wet sand. How tenderly those fingers could be when caressing a woman's body.

Flushing at the unbidden memory, Lorelei dragged her thoughts back to the present. "Oh, this is a ridiculous discussion. I don't give a hoot what you wear or what you do to your hands. Turn this thing around immediately and take me back to my wedding."

"Sorry, beautiful. That's something I'm not willing to do."

"Why not?" she demanded.

He looked at her then, and for once there was no laughter in those deep blue eyes. He was deadly serious—a rarity for Jack Storm. "Because, sweetheart, you promised a long time ago to marry me, and I've decided to hold you to that promise."

He'd shocked her. Jack knew it from the expression on her face, from the way she opened her mouth to say something, only to clamp it shut again without murmuring a word.

"You can't be serious," she finally managed to say.

"I assure you, I am." Despite the conviction in his voice, he hadn't been at all sure he could pull this off. Hell, he still wasn't sure he could pull it off. But his instinct—that same gut feeling that had saved his skin on treasure hunts more times than he cared to count—had told him he had to try. Because the moment he'd seen her again, he'd realized she was what had been missing in his life. Of all the treasures he'd discovered and lost through the years, she was the only one he'd regretted losing.

"That was ages ago. We were just kids."

"It was ten years ago, and there was nothing childlike about our relationship or the way we felt about each other. You gave yourself to me," Jack reminded her. "You said you loved me and promised to be my wife."

"I wasn't the one who forgot to show up for the wedding!"

Jack flushed, shame and regret reddening his face, his neck. "I was late. I—"

"You stood me up!"

"Lorelei, I—"

"I waited for you at that justice of the peace's house," she told him, her voice breaking. "I sat in a battered old chair in a dreary little room with the man's wife looking at me with pity in her eyes and I waited for you. I waited all that day and all that night. When the sun came up the next morning, I knew you weren't coming."

The pain in her voice felt like a one-two punch to his gut. Jack jerked the wheel of the truck to the right and pulled off onto the side of the road. He turned to her.

She looked away.

He felt the slam to his ribs again and knew he deserved it. "Lorelei, listen to me. I did come." Gently he turned her head so he could see her face—the face that had haunted him while he'd trekked through the jungles of Colombia, when he'd crossed the mountains of Peru, as he'd searched the floor of the Atlantic. A part of her had always stayed with him...kept him on course. He'd known that someday after he'd made his big strike, he would find her again and make things right. Only the years had somehow managed to slip by without him ever making that big strike. Then he'd walked into that bookstore and seen her again. He realized at once that she was not only still the love of his life, but she was his lady luck. With Lorelei beside him, he would find the treasure. Fate had brought her to him again, and he had never been one to question fate.

He looked into those whiskey-colored eyes, the siren's eyes he'd remembered filled with laughter, filled with love. But there was no laughter in those eyes now. There was no love. There was anger. And hurt. And he was the cause. Guilt washed over him, and for a moment he contemplated doing as she asked—taking her back to the church. No. He dismissed the notion. He couldn't let her marry another man.

He'd make it up to her, Jack promised himself. All he needed was a chance—the chance he'd stolen for himself today. "I came, Lorelei."

He saw the doubt, the questions as she narrowed her eyes

and searched his face. "It's true," he insisted. "I came the next afternoon. I was late. I'd been offered a chance to go out on a dive. There was this ship, part of a fleet of Spanish—"

She yanked away from his touch. "You jerk! You stupid, insensitive jerk! I lied to my parents and my sisters for you. I hurt them, telling them I didn't want to spend my spring vacation with them because I wanted to be with my friends. I hurt them deliberately so we could elope the way we'd planned. And now you tell me the reason I hurt them, the reason you left me waiting in that godforsaken little justice of the peace's office, was so that you could play treasure hunter?"

"I wasn't playing, Lorelei. I was on a diving boat. There was no way to get to a phone and call you."

"You didn't need a phone. You were supposed to be there!"

"I'm telling you I *was* there. But I was late. Sweetheart, I knew you were worried about the future, about how we would live."

"Do you blame me? Treasure hunting isn't exactly the most reliable profession."

He managed not to wince at the verbal cuff. "I wanted to surprise you with a stake," he said tightly, his own temper beginning to shred—partly out of anger, partly because he knew she was right. He'd had nothing to offer her ten years ago. He had little more now—except for the map and his gut feeling that he could find the mine. And that the mine would be the key to their future. "I earned nearly a thousand bucks on that dive. And I—"

"You nearly destroyed my life. I loved you, Jack. I loved you and trusted you. But all you cared about was finding some blasted treasure."

Her words carried the sting of a slap and took the edge off his temper. "Lorelei, that's not true. I—"

"I've had enough of this trip down memory lane with

you. I'm not interested in discussing it further," she said, her voice cool, her eyes even cooler. "I want you to take me back to the church so I can marry Herbert."

Jack recalled the sight of her standing in the back of the church, a vision dressed in white and looking so damn beautiful she'd stolen his breath away.

And she'd been about to marry another man.

He gritted his teeth. Shoving the truck into gear, he pulled out onto the road and stole a glimpse in his rearview mirror. The sprawl of the city dissolved behind them as he veered the Explorer east to the Highway 50 Loop and headed toward the Apache Trail and the Superstition Mountains.

"Jack, I said to turn around. Now. I want you to take me back to the church. I'm going to marry Herbert."

"Not if I can help it, you're not."

Two

"Jack, this is crazy. You can't just kidnap me from my wedding!"

"Sweetheart, I just did."

"Well, you certainly won't get away with it. As soon as Herbert finds out what's happened, he's going to come after me," Lorelei advised him, wishing she were half as sure of that as she sounded. Knowing Herbert, he'd probably be too busy calming his mother to worry about coming after her for quite some time.

"I wouldn't count on that if I were you. Somehow good old Herbert didn't strike me as the type of guy who's given to emotional reactions. If he were, he'd have decked me the minute he walked through the door of that bookstore and found me kissing you."

Lorelei flushed at the memory of looking up from the stack of books she'd been putting on a display and seeing Jack again. Her heart had seemed to stop working right then and there. In the years since he had jilted her, she'd seen him countless times in her dreams wearing that reckless smile, with that adventurous gleam in his blue eyes. Jack in the flesh was far more arresting than any dream had ever been. His smile was just as wicked and daring as she remembered; his eyes were just as blue. But there was a danger and a hardness in those eyes now that hadn't been there ten years ago. The body at twenty-three that she had found so sexy when they'd strolled hand in hand along the Florida beaches was even sexier now at thirty-three. The muscles were more defined, the deep bronze of his skin more weathered. The handsome boy she had fallen in love with had grown into a dangerously attractive man. Before she could stop herself, she'd said his name aloud.

In the blink of an eye, he'd been across the shop and had her in his arms. She hadn't been able to think or utter a reply of protest before his mouth was covering hers. The unexpected kiss had shattered her, so much so that she hadn't even heard the chime on the shop's door announcing someone's entrance. She hadn't heard anything at all until the sound of Herbert's shocked "Lorelei" had finally penetrated her senses. Of course, Herbert had immediately accepted her explanation that she and Jack were old friends. And instead of breaking Jack in two, he had shaken his hand.

"Besides, even if good old Herbert were to decide you needed rescuing," Jack continued, cutting into her thoughts, "my guess is that Desiree's story will put him off the notion."

Lorelei narrowed her eyes. "What story?"

"The one Desiree's probably telling him and your parents right about now."

"And just what exactly is it she's telling them?"

"That you and I were desperately in love ten years ago, but we were forced to separate when your parents moved away with you and your sisters."

"That is not the reason we split up, and you know it."

Ignoring her statement, he continued, "And when we ran into each other a few weeks ago, we both realized we still had feelings for one another and you began having second thoughts about marrying Herbert."

"I have *not* been having second thoughts about marrying Herbert," Lorelei insisted.

He cut her a glance. "Haven't you?"

"No. And Herbert will never believe that story. Neither will my parents. No one will."

"Not even when Desiree explains that you and I were engaged? That we had planned to elope until fate stepped in and kept us from carrying out our plans?"

"Fate had nothing to do with it," Lorelei argued. "And no one ever knew about our plans to elope. I never said a word about it to anyone—not even to my sisters."

"They know about it now," Jack replied. "I told Desiree the whole story a few days ago when I asked for her help. She was very sympathetic, I might add. Why do you think she agreed to help me?"

"Because Desiree's a soft touch and far too gullible for her own good." And she was going to murder her little sister the moment she got back to Mesa, Lorelei vowed silently. "Knowing your ability to spin tales, I have no doubt that you tricked her with all that talk about fate. She's a sucker for that romantic nonsense. Otherwise, she would never have done anything as stupid as this. Not if she knew the truth about what happened...the way you jilted me."

"I did *not* jilt you. I came, Lorelei," he repeated, his voice growing harder, his eyes heating. "I was late and by the time I got there, you were already gone. It was a mistake in judgment on my part—one that, believe me, I've lived to regret more than you can ever imagine. I would have explained everything to you if you hadn't been so stubborn and refused to take my phone calls."

"I wasn't interested in your explanations. If I had mattered to you, you would have been there."

"I tried—"

"The least you could have done was tell me to my face why you didn't show up." A part of her had prayed for weeks that he would come and do just that, make everything all right. But he hadn't.

"Don't you think I would have come to you if I could? I couldn't—at least not right away. The boat was leaving again that night. I planned to tell you and have you meet me later. By the time I got back and went to see you, to try to explain what had happened, it was too late. You were gone. Your family had packed up and moved somewhere on the West Coast." He shoved a hand through his hair. "I almost went crazy when I found you gone. I was going to explain everything to you, to try—"

Lorelei looked away. She hardened her heart, refusing to let herself be moved by his words. "No explanation was needed, Jack. Your absence said it all. There's certainly no need for excuses now."

"Damn it, Lorelei. If you'd just let me explain—"

She whipped around in her seat. "Save it, Jack! Whatever your reasons were, they're irrelevant now. You may have fooled Desiree with your lost-lovers story. But she's easily fooled. I'm not. And neither is Herbert. He won't believe a word of that story when he hears it."

"No?"

"No," Lorelei replied, tipping up her chin.

"Don't be so sure of that, sweetheart. A man is apt to do strange things when his pride's on the line. I should know. If I were Herbert and you disappeared on our wedding day and then I learned that the man you'd disappeared with was a man you'd once been engaged to, had even planned to elope with, then I'd have to ask myself why you'd insisted on a two-year engagement for us. And I'd also start asking myself why was it that you had once been so eager to marry someone else, yet the only reason there was a wedding scheduled today was because *I'd* been the one who'd insisted on it. Not you. Doesn't sound to me like you were all that anxious to marry the guy anyway."

Steaming over how much Desiree had revealed to Jack, Lorelei bit back an urge to scream. "That's the difference between you and Herbert. You have a suspicious, narrow mind. Herbert doesn't. He knows I love him and he trusts me."

"Does he?"

"Yes," Lorelei informed him.

"Then he's an even bigger fool than I thought he was."

"Herbert is not a fool. And he isn't going to believe a word of that story you have Desiree feeding everyone."

"You've obviously forgotten what a good actress your baby sister is. Take my word for it, she's *very* good."

It was true and she knew it. Desiree was born to be onstage. She'd been the only one of the three who had inherited any of their parents' theatrical talents.

"I caught her in a little dinner-theater number down in New Orleans not long ago. I went backstage to see her afterward. Did she happen to mention it to you?"

Desiree had told her about Jack's visit and his inquiries about her, but she had refused to listen. Just hearing Jack's name again had sent her into a tizzy of emotional confusion.

"She was very good in that play, and I imagine she'll be even more convincing when she talks to Herbert—especially since she can say with all honesty that you haven't been yourself at all lately. Certainly not the happy and eager bride-to-be."

"I *am* happy. Or at least I was until you pulled this stunt. And I'll have you know that I've been very much looking forward to marrying Herbert. I'm *still* looking forward to marrying him and I'm going to—just as soon as you take me back to Mesa."

"Trust me, Lorelei. When I take you back to Mesa, it won't be so you can marry Herbert."

Lorelei's pulse jumped at the possessive way he was looking at her. Chiding herself for her response, she looked out at the road ahead and forced herself to focus on her situation. Her thoughts immediately came back to her parents. "Regardless of what Desiree tells them, my parents are going to be worried."

"From what your mother told me, she's been worried over your lack of enthusiasm about marrying Herbert."

"How would you know what my mother's feeling?"

"Didn't I mention that I had breakfast with her and your dad a few days ago?"

"No, you didn't mention it." And neither had her parents.

He shrugged. "I ran into them in the hotel dining room. Seeing how we're old acquaintances, I thought asking them to join me was the polite thing to do. They really are a neat couple, you know. And of course, they insisted I come to the wedding."

Of course, her parents would invite him. It was their nature to do so. They were open and giving and always willing to share. "I'm sure the invitation would have been rescinded if they'd known what you'd planned."

Color climbed up his neck and cheeks. "I'm hoping that given the circumstances, they'll understand I couldn't very well tell them what my plans were. On the other hand, I don't think they'll be all that surprised."

"You don't think they'll be surprised that you kidnapped me on my wedding day?"

"Your mother won't. According to her, you moped around for weeks after your family moved to the West Coast. She assumed I was the reason. She said you never said anything, but she suspected you and I had been in love and that you were missing me." He slanted her a glance. "Did you miss me, Lorelei?"

"As I said before, I was little more than a child. You were my first case of puppy love."

He flashed her a look that had Lorelei pressing her back against the seat. It was there again, that reckless danger she'd sensed in him earlier. "Don't kid yourself, Lorelei. Neither one of us were children, and what we felt for one another was very real. You loved me with a woman's heart and a woman's body. And I loved you the same way." He paused. His expression grew even more somber. "I still love you. I always have."

Lorelei's breath lodged in her throat. An invisible fist seemed to tighten around her heart and refused to let go. She felt herself weakening. "Jack—"

The blare of a horn from an oncoming car sounded. Jack swore and jerked his attention back to the road. He yanked on the wheel of the truck and brought it back into the proper lane.

Her heart still pounding, Lorelei crushed a handful of satin in her fist. She refused to let him do this to her, to make her feel anything for him again. He was a charmer, she reminded herself as Jack slowed the vehicle and began easing over onto the side of the road. Hadn't she even told him once that if he'd lived in another lifetime, he'd have been a pirate? Only he'd have been a pirate who would have charmed the ships' passengers out of their gold instead of stealing it from them.

She wasn't the same naive girl who'd believed his lies of love ten years ago. She was older, smarter and she wouldn't allow him to charm his way back into her life.

The tires crunched on the gravel as he brought the truck to a halt on the road's shoulder. He turned to face her. "Lorelei, I want another chance."

She heard the plea in his voice, saw it in his eyes. She closed her heart to both. She'd taken a chance by loving him once, and it had nearly destroyed her. She wouldn't, couldn't make that mistake again. "A chance to do what, Jack? To hurt me again?"

She caught his slight wince, but forced herself to remain

strong. She'd vowed ten years ago not to leave herself open to that kind of pain ever again. She'd opted for safe. Allowing Jack Storm back into her life was anything but safe.

"A chance to prove to you that I'm the right man for you—not Herbert."

"You're wrong."

"I don't think so. And judging from that kiss we shared two weeks ago, I think you know it, too. Ten years may have passed, but nothing's changed between us. All that fire, that passion we felt before...it's still there between us. Only you're too stubborn to admit it."

Her heart picked up speed at the mention of the kiss, at the seductive warmth in his eyes. No, she would not subject herself to that craziness again. Forcing her voice to remain even, Lorelei said, "You're the one who's being stubborn, Jack. I told you, I'm in love with Herbert—not you."

She saw fire flash in his blue eyes and before she could think of moving, he'd snapped the release on his seat belt and was reaching for her. "Jack, no."

"Yes," he said as he cupped her head with both hands and eased his fingers into the tumbled mass of curls. "I have to. I have to."

And then he was lowering his head, covering her mouth with his. Slowly, oh so slowly, his lips brushed against hers. Teasing. Tempting. His tongue traced the seam of her mouth, and a shiver of longing shimmied through her. He repeated the movement, and Lorelei could feel her control slipping as her world started to tilt.

He lifted his head a moment, looked into her eyes. "Lorelei. My sweet, lovely Lorelei," he whispered, "I love you."

When his lips touched hers again, her eyes drifted closed. A mistake, she realized too late as the sensations grew more intense. His tongue caressed her mouth, over and over again. And when he sought entry once more, she opened to him like a flower to sunshine.

Jack groaned. She felt a shudder race through him as she touched her tongue to his. And then he was crushing her to him and deepening the kiss.

The kiss went on forever as he continued to taste her, to worship her with his mouth and his tongue. His hands skimmed over her neck, her shoulders, the curve of her breasts. Lorelei gasped when he cupped the fullness in his palms and she strained against the confines of the seat-belt harness, wanting to be closer, wanting him to touch her, wanting to touch him.

Jack lifted his head and caught her face in his hands. "God, how I've missed you. When I think how close I came to losing you forever." His voice trembled, and he pulled her to him.

Lorelei buried her face against his chest, breathing in the scent of mountain air, of sweat, of Jack. It felt so right being in his arms again, to feel the steady thudding of his heart beneath her palm.

"We were meant to be together, Lorelei. I'm sure of it. Fate caused that map to land in my hands so I would come here and find you again."

Lorelei blinked, struggling to clear her kiss-drugged brain and make sense out of what he was saying. Map? "What map?"

"To the gold mine."

"The gold mine?" she repeated.

"Yes. If I hadn't won the map in that card game, I might never have come to Arizona. And by the time I got around to finding you again, it would have been too late. You would have already been married to Herbert."

Lorelei stiffened. *He was here because of a gold mine?* Oh, dear God, what a fool she was. What had she been thinking to kiss him like that? To even listen to him. She could not do this to herself, she decided, and pulled free of his arms.

"What's wrong?" he asked, lines of concern etching his face.

"I'm an idiot. That's what's wrong. For even listening to you. I must be out of my mind to even be here like this with you. I don't know what I was thinking. Whatever there was between us...whatever we had is over. It's in the past. We can't go back, Jack. I don't *want* to go back." She didn't want the mad whirlwind of emotions that went with loving Jack Storm. There were too many highs and lows, too much uncertainty. She swallowed and forced her voice to be firm as she said, "I'm not the same lovesick girl you once knew. That Lorelei Mason no longer exists. I have a new life—a life I'm happy with. And it doesn't include you."

Anger. She saw it catch like blue flames in his eyes. A day's growth of stubble darkened his chin. A muscle ticked furiously in his lean jaw as she watched him strap on his seat belt. "You're wrong. The Lorelei Mason I knew and loved is still there inside you. You may have buried her, buried her really deep, but she's still there. You wiped away any doubts that I might have had on that score just now when you kissed me back." He wrapped his hands around the steering wheel and turned to look at her. Once again Lorelei was struck by the element of danger that seemed to be so much a part of him now. "We belong together, Lorelei, and I intend to prove it to you."

"How?" Lorelei asked as he shifted the gears and pulled the Explorer back onto the road.

"By doing what I should have done ten years ago, what I would have done if we'd gotten married like we planned. I'm taking you with me."

Lorelei's pulse stuttered as she recalled the foolish plans they had made. She had been so in love with him, she'd become caught up in the tales of adventure he'd spun of the two of them traveling the world together and searching for lost treasures. It had been a fool's dream, a girl's dream that she'd buried when he'd broken her heart and left her standing at the altar.

But as the truck sped down the road, Lorelei noticed for the first time the changing landscape. The stretch of highway from the city of Mesa had given way to open desert and rocky, low hills. She'd known they'd been going east but only now did she realize where they were headed. Steep river canyons sprawled out before them, and the rugged face of the Superstition Mountains filled the horizon like a temple of some ancient god. "Jack, you can't be serious."

"Oh, but I am, sweetheart," he said as he veered on the road toward the sign that read Apache Junction. "I once told you that beneath that prim and proper girl I fell in love with there was an adventuress waiting to be set free. She's still there, buried a little deeper maybe, but she's there. And I intend to find her again."

"Jack, really—"

"I promised you once that if you married me, someday we'd strike it rich and I'd lay gold at your feet. I'm going to keep my promise, Lorelei."

She recalled the crazy promise he'd made when he'd proposed to her. It had been the rash promise of a reckless adventurer who thought the world was his for the taking. "And just how do you plan to do that? Rob a bank?"

"I'll do better than that. I'm going to find the Lost Dutchman's Gold Mine."

"You're crazy."

"And you're going to help me."

"You really are out of your mind if that's what you think."

Obviously ignoring her, he continued, "And once we find that mine, my sweet siren, I'm going to hold you to your promise to marry me."

"You've got to be joking."

"I never joke when it comes to hunting treasure. You

know that." In fact, it was the one thing, maybe the only thing in his life, that he'd taken seriously. He had realized from the time he was ten and his father had taken him diving near the site of a sunken Spanish galleon, that searching for treasure was what he wanted to do with his life. Jack had known in his gut that there was treasure still hidden inside that old ship. But his father had shaken his head and motioned for him to follow him and the others back to the surface.

But he hadn't listened to his father. He'd followed his gut instead and dove deeper into the stern of the ship. And he had been right. When his head broke the surface of the water, he'd held a fistful of gold doubloons in his bag. He could still remember the expression on his father's face—a mixture of pride and concern.

"That's a brave lad you've got there, Jamie." The old salt named Murphy slapped his father on the back. "Puts the rest of us to shame."

"Aye, don't I know it. The boy has no fear. Worries me some that he might get the fever."

Murphy laughed. "What do you expect? The boy's got yer blood flowing in his veins, don't he?"

"True. True. But I promised his mother that I'd see to it the boy would have more out of life than this. A man wants more than a life spent hunting for treasure for his only son."

And his father had tried, Jack admitted. He'd forced him to go to school and even insisted he attend college. But when Jamie Storm had lost his life in a diving accident, Jack's world had fallen apart. He'd dropped out of college, tried unsuccessfully to get on with some of the treasure-hunting outfits and somehow ended up in the navy. Six months after his stint was over, he'd still been floundering—until he'd met Lorelei. When he'd seen her on the beach that first time, there had been that same rush of excitement he'd experienced the day he'd discovered the gold doubloons. And just as his gut had told him there was treasure still buried in that sunken ship, his gut told him Lorelei herself was a treasure—a treasure meant for him.

Meeting her had been the turning point for him. He'd been alive again for the first time since his father's death. His luck and life had changed after that. He'd gotten on with a treasure-hunting crew and made his first big find.

And lost Lorelei in the process. Nothing had been quite the same since. Until he'd won the treasure map and fate had brought her back into his life. Now that he'd found her again, he had no intention of letting her go. But first he had to convince her that it was with him that she belonged.

"Jack, are you listening to me?"

Jack dragged his thoughts back to the present at the angry note in Lorelei's voice. "Sorry. What did you say?"

"I asked you why are you doing this? What could you possibly hope to prove by dragging me off to the mountains with you to search for some gold mine that probably doesn't even exist?"

"Oh, it exists, all right. And I've got the map to her."

"Then go find the blasted mine. You don't need me."

"That's where you're wrong. I do need you."

"You don't even know me anymore."

"I know enough. Enough to realize that you don't belong buried away in some little desert town married to a banker."

"Herbert and I happen to love each other."

"Right. That's why when he kissed you goodbye that day at the bookstore, the two of you generated about as much heat as a soggy newspaper and a wet match."

Lorelei flushed. Her brown eyes sparked with temper. "We were in a public place."

"It didn't stop the sparks from flying between you and me. The air sizzled between us, just like it always does. Just like it did a few minutes ago."

"There's more to a relationship and a marriage than sex.

Herbert and I respect one another. We share similar interests and goals,'' she defended.

''Sounds more like a business agreement than a marriage if you ask me.''

''No one *asked* you,'' she said with heat in her voice. ''This conversation is ridiculous. This whole situation is ridiculous. It's insane. *You're* insane!''

Jack shrugged. ''Maybe I am. But I know what I feel in my gut. I feel the same thing now that I felt when I saw you for the first time ten years ago, the same thing that I felt when I saw you standing in that bookstore two weeks ago.''

''Which is what? Wait.'' She held up her hand. ''Let me guess. You feel it's fate, right? That you and I belong together.''

''Yes.''

''That's the same tired line you used on me when I met you on the beach for the first time. Well, it may have worked ten years ago on a naive eighteen-year-old girl, but it doesn't hold water with a twenty-eight-year-old woman. I'm not buying it this time, Jack. And I'm not buying this crazy treasure-hunting scheme of yours, either.''

''Go ahead, make fun if you want to, but it doesn't change anything. I know we *are* going to find the Lost Dutchman's Mine. Just like I know in my gut that it's not Herbert you should be marrying, but me.'' He shifted the truck into third gear as they climbed deeper into the heart of the mountains. ''And I promise you, by the time we leave these mountains, you're going to know it, too.''

Turning the truck to the left, he followed the sign pointing to the Goldfield Ghost Town and silently prayed that he was right.

Lorelei sharpened her gaze as Jack turned off the main road and drove down the street of what appeared to be another Western town. ''Oh, great,'' she quipped, breaking the stony silence she'd adapted for the past twenty miles. "What is this place, another ghost town?" She'd been fascinated at the sight of the old Goldfield Ghost Town, which they had passed through earlier, but not for the life of her would she let Jack know it, nor would she ask him a single question about the odd little place.

"We're in the town of Tortilla Flats. Population six. It used to be a road camp for work crews on the Salt River Project around the turn of the century. Now it's more or less a watering hole and tourist stop for travelers along the Apache Trail."

Lorelei stared at the strange collection of buildings that appeared to lean against one another for support. Although she'd lived in Arizona for the past four years, she had never visited a single one of these little towns. Yet Jack seemed to know all about them. Spotting a sign that boasted Jacob Waltz Enjoyed Tortilla Flat's Home Cookin, she said, "Well, I guess *that* explains how you know so much about this place. Evidently you stumbled across it while searching for the Dutchman's fictitious gold mine."

"The gold mine exists, Lorelei. As far as that sign, I'm afraid it's false advertising. This place didn't even exist when old Jacob was searching the mountains for gold. As far as the food, it's pretty good. The restaurant up ahead serves great burgers and chili."

Just the mention of food, and Lorelei's stomach grumbled. Suddenly she realized she hadn't eaten a thing since the buttered toast with coffee she'd had before lunch that day. Given her wedding had been scheduled as a late-afternoon affair and it was already after six in the evening, it had been a good eight hours since she'd eaten.

"I don't know about you, but I'm starved. I thought we'd stop and get something to eat here."

"I'd rather be eating the food I selected for my wedding reception."

"Sorry, but that's not an option." Jack pulled the Explorer to a stop in front of an Old West saloon and turned to her. "This is probably going to be the last home-cooked meal either of us has for a while. I'd hate to see you refuse it just to spite me."

"I have no intention of refusing it. The way I see it, I'm going to need all my strength if I'm going to find my way down this blasted mountain and back to Mesa."

Slowly, lazily, Jack wrapped and unwrapped his powerful hands around the steering wheel. "You're not going to have to find your way back to Mesa. I'm going to take you there myself—after we find the mine."

When she started to object, Jack lifted his hand and touched her face, his voice dropping to a whisper as he said, "Don't fight me on this, Lorelei."

Lorelei turned away from him. She'd always been too susceptible to that combination of recklessness and tenderness in him.

Jack sighed and dropped his hand. "In addition to eating, I thought you might want to change into something a little more comfortable for traveling. The road's going to get a lot bumpier about five miles past here."

"That's very considerate of you," she said with mock sweetness. "But since I was expecting to be at my wedding reception now and not stuck up here in the mountains with you, I'm afraid I didn't happen to bring along a change of clothes."

"That's okay. I had Desiree pack some things for you," he said, chuckling at her sarcasm. "You'll find jeans, shirts and hiking boots in the bag behind your seat."

One more thing to take her sister to task for, Lorelei decided as Jack got out of the truck and came around to open the door for her. Lorelei glared at him as he helped her down from the truck's high seat. The hem of her wedding gown and train spilled out of the vehicle behind her and onto the street, stirring up a small cloud of red-colored dust that promptly attached itself to the satin. Lorelei jerked the train of the gown up and draped it over one arm.

After retrieving the bag from behind her seat, Jack took her arm. He motioned to the restaurant. "You can change clothes while I order us something to eat."

He acted as though it was the most natural thing in the world for the two of them to waltz into town with her dressed in a wedding gown and he in his jeans. Feeling conspicuous as glances were cast their way, Lorelei said, "I hate to point out the obvious, but don't you think anyone's going to notice the fact that I'm wearing a wedding dress?"

"I think it'd be hard for them not to notice. You make a beautiful bride."

"That's not what I meant," she said, and fought the urge to stamp her foot.

"I know what you meant. But as I said, there's only six people who actually live in this little town. The rest are just tourists or workers. I've gotten to be friends with the locals during the past couple of weeks—including the people who own the restaurant. And I doubt they'll be surprised at all since they're expecting us."

"What do you mean they're expecting us?"

Jack shrugged. "I mentioned that I was getting married soon and that my bride and I would be spending our honeymoon in the mountains. I told them we'd try to stop by on our way up the mountain."

Lorelei stopped in the middle of street. "And they believed you?"

"Sure," he said, flashing her a smile. "What's not to believe?"

"Besides the foolish notion that I'd agree to spend my honeymoon in these mountains, there's the absurd idea that I'd even consider marrying you."

"I don't see anything absurd about it. You did agree to marry me—"

"Ten years ago," she reminded him.

"So we've had a long engagement. Lots of couples do."

"We are not engaged," she insisted.

"As far as I'm concerned, we are. You never officially broke the engagement. And I've still got the wedding bands we picked out." Putting down the suitcase, he shoved his hand inside his pants pocket. He pulled out a jeweler's pouch and emptied its contents into the palm of his other hand. Two thin, shiny gold bands winked at her.

Lorelei swallowed past the thickness in her throat as she remembered the two of them selecting the rings from a small jewelry store in Fort Lauderdale. "You kept them?"

"Of course."

"But why?" she finally managed to ask.

"Because I never stopped loving you. It was always my plan to find you again someday, for the two of us get married. I just hadn't expected it to take so long." He dumped the rings back into their pouch and tucked the little bag into his pocket.

And there had been a time ten years ago when she had hoped he would find her, soothe away her hurt and make everything right again. But all that had changed after…after…

"Remember the honeymoon we'd planned?"

Lorelei pulled her thoughts away from those dreadful weeks right after he had failed to show up for their wedding. She squeezed her eyes shut a moment against the remembered pain, the fear.

"We were going to go diving off the coast near the site of that sunken ship, remember? It would have been your first treasure dive. I'll never forget how excited you were…."

She *had* been excited—at the thought of being married to Jack, at the prospect of doing something so daring as diving for lost treasure. The idea had appealed to an adventurous streak in her that she hadn't even known existed.

But then, Jack himself had appealed to that same reckless streak. Looking at him now, his eyes glowing with excitement, she found it was easy to remember those dreams and plans. It was easy to remember how deeply she had loved him.

"Don't you see? Trying to locate the Dutchman's Mine will be the same thing. Only instead of searching in the ocean for treasure, we'll be searching in the mountains."

Lorelei felt herself tempted. It would be all too easy and terribly foolish to allow herself to be sucked into those fantasies again. "I'm not interested in searching for any gold mine."

"But you will be," he told her as he urged her toward the restaurant. "There's more of the old Lorelei in you than you'd like to admit."

Jerking her arm free, she marched into the restaurant in front of him. Lorelei blinked as her eyes adjusted to the darker interior. She scanned the Old Western–style restaurant with its wooden tables and ladder-back chairs. When she felt Jack come to stand beside her, she asked, "What's to stop me from telling these people the truth? That you kidnapped me and brought me here against my will."

"Go ahead. Just don't expect anyone to believe you. I already told the owners that you were quite a joker. Besides, the wife of the man who runs the place thinks I'm quite a catch."

"I'll bet."

"Jack," the dark-haired woman behind the counter called out. "And this must be your lovely bride."

"Hello, Isabel. You're looking as gorgeous as ever, I see." He gave her a kiss on the cheek. "Sure you don't want to ditch Alberto and run away with me?"

The woman flushed and gave Jack a smack. "Behave yourself, Bandito, and introduce me to your wife."

"Isabel, this is Lorelei. Lorelei, Isabel."

"She's as beautiful as you said she was. Welcome to

Tortilla Flats, Lorelei." She gave Lorelei a welcoming hug and nearly squeezed the stuffing out of her before she released her. "You've landed yourself quite an hombre here. But I suspect you know that already."

"I—"

"Order's ready," someone called out from the kitchen. "Jack, *mi amigo.*" A dark-eyed man with graying hair waved in greeting. "So you convinced her to come with you to our mountains after all."

"*Bueno,* Alberto. Yes, I convinced her to come," Jack returned.

"I will fix something special for you and your bride, then. Isabel, show Jack and his lady to a table and then come help Maria."

Isabel muttered something in Spanish and rolled her eyes heavenward. "Jack, you and your Lorelei sit over there away from that racket. I will come back in a minute to take your orders. Right now I'd better help Maria before those little devils tear the place apart."

Lorelei looked across the room to where a couple with five youngsters had their hands full trying to keep their troops seated. Her gaze shifted to the trays Isabel and another woman were carrying to the table. Lorelei's mouth watered at the smell of burgers and bowls of steaming chili.

"The ladies' room is down the hall, first door on your left," Jack informed her. He held out the suitcase with her clothes. When Lorelei reached for it, he held on to it a moment longer. "Just in case you're thinking of trying to find a back door to sneak out of, I'll save you the trouble of looking. There isn't one. And if you're not back here in exactly fifteen minutes, I'll come looking for you."

Lorelei yanked the suitcase from him and flounced off down the narrow hallway. She paused a moment before the door marked Ladies and glanced back in the direction from which she'd come. Jack stood there watching her. With his feet spread apart, the light from the dining room casting shadows across his unsmiling face, he looked every inch the dangerous pirate she'd accused him of being. Tipping up her chin, Lorelei pushed open the door and stepped inside the bathroom.

The place was small but clean. Two stalls took up most of the space. A single basin with a small square mirror positioned above it filled one corner of the room. A countertop no more than a dozen inches wide ran across the back wall. An oval-shaped mirror sat in a stand to one side. Centered four feet above the counter was a narrow window that she judged to be only a fraction wider than her hips. *What I wouldn't do to have Clea's slim hips right now,* Lorelei thought. If she ditched the wedding dress, she might just be able to make it. But she'd have to hurry.

Moving quickly, Lorelei hoisted the suitcase onto the countertop and pulled out a pair of jean shorts, T-shirt and the hiking boots. She frowned as she thought of Desiree packing her things without her even knowing it. She'd deal with her little sister once she got back to Mesa, Lorelei promised herself. Kicking off her ivory pumps, she reached for the hooks and detached the train at the back of her dress. Bundling up the length of satin, she stuffed it in the top of the suitcase, then went to work on the tiny satin-covered buttons that ran down the back of her dress.

Several minutes later her arms ached from stretching behind her, and she had succeeded in opening no more than a half dozen of the buttons. Frustrated, Lorelei strained against the fabric, trying to pop the buttons free. It was no use. The things didn't budge, let alone break loose. *Oh, God. What possessed me to buy a dress with so many stupid buttons?*

Because you hadn't planned on unbuttoning them yourself, Lorelei reminded herself. At least that's what Desiree had said when she'd encouraged her to buy the dress. Yet for the life of her, she had to admit that she hadn't experienced any great anticipation at having Herbert undo them for her, either.

Lorelei glanced at her watch. Twelve minutes. She'd been gone twelve minutes already, she realized. Jack would come looking for her any moment now, and she hadn't even managed to change clothes yet, let alone escape through the window. Arching her shoulders, she strained to break the buttons free.

She heard a tap at the door. "Lorelei?"

"Go away," she told Jack.

"What's taking you so long?"

"Nothing. I'll be there in a few minutes."

She took a deep breath and arched her back and shoulders again. Nothing. Zip. Nada. The dratted things were evidently sewn on with steel thread.

"Need some help?"

Lorelei jumped at the nearness of his voice. She glanced up in the mirror and saw Jack standing behind her, an odd expression on his face. "I can't unbutton the stupid dress."

"Want me to do it for you?" he asked, a smile sneaking across his mouth. "At the rate you're going, you'll be lucky to get changed before breakfast."

Too irritated to speak, she whipped her hair around to fall across her shoulder and offered him her back.

The breath stilled in her chest as Jack moved closer and began to unfasten the buttons. One. Two. Three. Four. She could feel his fingers moving down her back, slipping the buttons free from the satin loops. His fingers brushed along her bare skin and sent sensation skipping down her spine. Lorelei closed her eyes and bit down on her bottom lip to keep silent.

"You always had the most beautiful skin. The color of cream."

"I have freckles," she somehow managed to reply.

"Only a few." He slipped open another two buttons and skimmed the backs of his fingers against her bare flesh.

"So soft. Like silk. Sometimes when I'd be out at sea, I'd lie awake nights and look up at the sky and remember how soft and beautiful your skin was."

Lorelei caught the note of longing in his voice. Glancing up, she discovered him watching her in the mirror. The last of the buttons were freed, and her dress fell from her shoulders to her waist, leaving her breasts hidden only by the thin strapless bra.

Jack lifted his gaze to meet hers.

Her breath hitched. She couldn't move as she watched desire flare in his eyes.

"Lorelei," he whispered before lowering his mouth to her shoulder.

Lorelei gasped as first Jack's lips and then his tongue touched her shoulder. The feeling was so erotic, yet so familiar. A surge of longing raced through her.

"Come on, Sarah, let Mommy wash your—" The door to the bathroom burst open, and the mother of the five children stood there staring at them. She started to back out of the room. "Oh, my. I'm so sorry. I thought this was the ladies' room."

"It is," Jack said, spinning around to stand in front of Lorelei like a shield. "I was just helping my wife with her dress. We'll be out of your way in a moment. I'll wait for you at the table, sweetheart."

Once he was gone, Lorelei avoided the other woman's knowing eyes and scurried into one of the stalls to change. Dear God, what had she been thinking of? Lorelei asked herself as she stepped out of the gown and threw it across the bathroom door. She pulled off the silk nylons and tossed them over the gown. Hurrying, she shrugged into her shorts and pulled on the T-shirt. She had to get away, Lorelei told herself as she sat on the toilet seat and slipped on her socks and hiking boots. And she had to do it now.

Lorelei remained in the stall until she heard the woman and the little girl leave. When she was alone again, she pushed her suitcase aside and hopped up on top of the counter. Using the heel of her hand, she shoved against the worn window lock. Finally it opened. She pulled up once, twice, cursing when she broke a nail. Determined, she tried again and the window finally came free. The sky was already growing dark, and Lorelei could feel the slap of heat as she shoved the window up to the top.

A bead of perspiration trickled between her breasts. Her heart pumped furiously as she hurried to place first one leg and then the other through the window's small opening. Taking another deep breath, she leapt to the ground, stumbled and landed on her bottom.

She'd made it. She was free, Lorelei thought as she scrambled to stand up.

"Going somewhere?" Jack asked as he stepped out of the shadows to stand in front of her.

Three

Lorelei swatted his hand away and pushed herself up to her feet. She glared at him while dusting off the seat of her jean shorts. "How did you know?"

"I saw the window, too. It wasn't hard to figure out that you'd try to make a run for it." He paused. "And since you don't have any money or credit cards on you, just what were you planning to do? Walk down the mountain?"

"If I had to," she said, her voice defiant. "I was hoping to hitch a ride."

His amusement fizzled at her reply. Fury at her recklessness exploded inside him. Before he could stop himself, Jack grabbed her by the arms, wanting to shake her. "You little idiot. Don't you know how dangerous that would have been? Do you have any idea what position you could have found yourself in? What if you'd gotten hurt or even gotten yourself lost trying to find your way down the mountain? And what's to stop some crazy from offering you a ride and then doing God knows what to you?"

Just the thought of something happening to her made Jack ill. He pulled her stiff body into his arms. "I want you to promise me you won't try something stupid like this again."

At her silence, Jack set her at arm's length. "I mean it, Lorelei. I want your promise that you won't try to run away again."

"I'm not promising you anything," she told him. "Because the minute I get another chance, I'm going to take it and go back to Mesa."

Disappointed in her response, Jack sighed as he stared into her eyes, caught that glint of steel beneath the warmth. Lord, but the woman was stubborn. Much more stubborn than she'd been ten years ago. But somehow he'd get through that stubborn streak of hers. Somehow he'd prove to her that the old Lorelei was still very much alive and that she belonged with him.

He simply had to, Jack told himself. Because without her, the life that stretched out before him seemed very empty. "Then I guess I'll have to see that you don't get another chance." Putting an arm around her stiff shoulders, he led her around front to where he'd parked the Explorer.

"Where are we going?" she asked when he opened the door and motioned for her to get inside. "I thought we were going to eat dinner?"

"I assumed you weren't hungry when you did your vanishing act back there. Or hadn't you thought that far ahead?"

"I'm starving and you know it. I'm not going anywhere until I get something to eat."

He almost laughed out loud at the petulant look on her face. He kissed her forehead instead and earned himself another scowl. "Don't worry, sweetheart. I intend to feed you. But you'll have to wait about twenty minutes."

"Why?" she demanded, narrowing her eyes.

"Because I don't like driving on these roads at night,

and we didn't get nearly as far up in the mountains today as I'd planned. Too bad you didn't decide on a morning wedding."

"Believe me, if I had known about *your* plans, I would have scheduled a night wedding," she replied sassily.

"I don't doubt that for a minute. Now get in the truck, or I'll put you in it myself. Come to think of it," Jack said, dropping his voice as he rubbed his jaw and allowed his gaze to sweep over her, "maybe that's not such a bad idea."

Lorelei scrambled into her seat. "Where are we going?"

"Not far. We'll be spending the night in a little cabin about ten miles from here. I'm hoping to make it there before full darkness sets in."

"When did you rent a cabin?"

"I didn't. It belongs to Isabel and Alberto. They use it as a little hideaway when they want to get away from the business and town. They've offered us the use of it for our wedding night."

"This is not our wedding night. You and I are not married."

"I'll be happy to remedy that situation anytime you give me the word."

"Don't hold your breath."

Letting her rebuff bounce off of him, Jack reached for her seat belt. "Need some help buckling up?" He started to pull it across her breasts.

Lorelei snatched the strap from his hand and did the honors herself. "What about my suitcase? And my wedding gown? I left them in the bathroom."

"I know." Jack shut the truck's door and went around to the other side. He climbed into the driver's seat and strapped on his seat belt.

"That dress was very expensive and I want it."

"What for?"

"Because I intend to use it again—when I get back to Mesa and marry Herbert."

Gritting his teeth, Jack turned to her. "If you wear that dress again," he began, calmly measuring his words despite the jealousy clawing at him, "it won't be to marry Herbert."

"Jack, I want my dress and suitcase."

He started the engine. "They're already in the truck. I had Isabel and Alberto's son store them in the back, along with our dinner." He put the Explorer into reverse and sent the tires spinning up a cloud of dust.

For a moment she remained silent, seeming to mull over his comment. "What did you tell them? Isabel and Alberto, I mean. How did you explain my not coming back into the restaurant to eat dinner?"

"I already told you that they think you're a bit of a jokester. As far as they're concerned, your sneaking out the window was just another one of your pranks." Jack slanted her a glance as he shifted the truck into gear. "Besides, I told them you weren't interested in eating. You were much more anxious to get to the wedding night."

Lorelei's face turned a pretty shade of pink, just as he knew it would. "How could you?"

"Easy," he said, smiling at her horrified expression. "After helping you out of that wedding dress, I just went with the way I was feeling. They seemed to understand."

Giving him a stony look, Lorelei crossed her arms over her chest and stared straight ahead.

It was true, Jack admitted to himself. Helping Lorelei out of her wedding dress had been a mixture of heaven and hell. And had left his body and mind whirling with fantasies about her. Just remembering the way she'd looked with her cheeks flushed, her hair tumbling about her shoulders, her eyes bright with feminine awareness had his jeans growing uncomfortably snug again. If only she really were his bride and this really were their wedding night.

It was a start, Jack told himself. She desired him, and knowing Lorelei, desire didn't come without emotion. Desire would have to be enough for now. If he could make Lorelei want him, he could make her love him again. He patted his pocket, felt the pouch with the wedding bands. She was his luck, his siren who would lead him to the treasure. And once he had the treasure, he could go to her deserving of her love. He would have something more to offer her than just himself and his dreams. He could offer her a future.

If he found the mine, it would give him the start he wanted for them. He could buy that little boat-sales-and-repair outfit back in Florida where he'd been working off and on for the past five years. He enjoyed the work, was good at it and the old guy who owned it had already offered it to him twice. He'd buy it, Jack decided, warming to the idea. He'd put down the roots that were so important to Lorelei. But first he needed to find the mine, Jack reminded himself. Because despite what he'd told Lorelei, he couldn't marry her now—not without that stake for their future.

The truck hit a hole in the road, and Lorelei bounced around in her seat. "You weren't kidding about these roads being bumpy," she said.

"I'm afraid this is the easy part. Tomorrow's when it's going to get rough."

"Rougher than this?" Lorelei asked, and groaned as they hit another bone-jarring rut in the road. She moved her jaw experimentally to be sure she hadn't lost any teeth.

"The cabin's just a little ways ahead on the right. Alberto said we'd be able to see the chimney from the distance."

But the sky in the distance was quickly growing dark. "I think that's it." Lorelei pointed past a solitary paloverde to a tier of the rust-colored, igneous rock jutting up into the night sky.

"I think you're right."

The tires of the Explorer crunched along the gravel road as Jack guided the vehicle over another series of ruts before coming to a halt in front of a small, rustic-looking cabin. "You stay here while I open the place up and crank up the generator out back."

A sliver of moonlight and the headlights of the Explorer were the only relief from the ever blackening skyline. The Superstition Mountains loomed in the distance, looking dangerous and foreboding. Suddenly Lorelei was conscious of just how alone she was sitting in the Explorer. She got out of the truck to stretch her muscles, now sore from the rough ride. Something rattled in the brush two feet away, and Lorelei jumped, her heartbeat picking up speed. The devil with this, she thought. She was getting back in the truck. Opening the door, she started to climb inside when an animal's howl pierced the quiet night. No way was she staying out here by herself. Slamming the door shut, Lorelei ran toward the back of the cabin in search of Jack.

"Jack," she called out as she hurried along the side of the cabin. "Jack, where are y—?" Lorelei whirled around at the sound of something behind her and cried out as the shadows moved. She screamed and started to run when a pair of arms snagged her around the waist. Letting out a bloodcurdling scream, she started to kick.

"For God's sake, Lorelei. It's me. It's Jack."

She went still. "Jack?"

"Yes."

She turned around in his arms so that she could see his face. She looked up into those midnight blue eyes, saw the frown knotting across his forehead. Her entire body went limp. She didn't stop to think; she simply leaned against him, wrapped her arms around him and held on.

"Hey, it's okay, sweetheart. It's okay. What happened?

Something spook you?'' he asked, his voice calm and soothing as he rubbed his hand up and down her spine.

''I...I heard something moving around in the bushes.''

''Probably just a lizard or gecko.''

''And then there was this terrible howling.'' She shivered and burrowed closer to him.

''It was just a coyote.''

Lorelei's body went still. ''A coyote? You mean, there are coyotes out here?''

''Sure. There's quite a few of them in the mountains. But it's okay. You don't have to worry about them bothering you. They don't usually come around the cabins.''

''I think one of them changed his mind. He sounded really close, Jack. I think he was right out front in that cluster of trees behind the truck.''

''I doubt that. But even if he was, it's nothing to worry about.''

''Nothing to worry about? He could have killed me.''

He set her away from him. ''Lorelei,'' he began in that calm, reasoning tone of his, ''unless you've got a hen or a rabbit I don't know about, the coyote isn't going to bother you. You don't have a hen or a rabbit in that suitcase of yours, do you?''

''You know I don't.''

''Then you don't have anything to worry about. No coyote's going to be brave enough to come snooping around this cabin tonight.''

As if on cue, the coyote let out another eerie howl, and Lorelei jumped right back into Jack's arms. ''Well, I think that fellow is braver than you think.''

Jack's chest started to shake, and Lorelei lifted her head. With the aid of the moonlight, she could just make out the twitch of his lips as he tried to hold back his laughter.

''You jerk.'' She punched his shoulder. ''You think it's funny? I'm standing here scared half to death we're going to be attacked by some wild animal, and you find it amusing?"

"I'm sorry. Really, I am." He swallowed, obviously trying to look serious. He failed big time as far as she was concerned. "It's just that..." The laughter won, and he let out a chuckle.

"This isn't funny, Jack."

"I know." He ran his hand over his face evidently in an effort to wipe the grin from his mouth. He barely succeeded. Even if his mouth was no longer smiling, his eyes were. "I didn't mean to laugh at you. It's just that since you've lived in Arizona for a while, I just assumed you'd be used to some of the common sounds of the desert."

"I don't live in the desert. I live in the city," she informed him. It didn't matter that between one half to two-thirds of the state was made up of desert, depending on which definition of "desert" the scientists decided to use. She wasn't about to admit that to Jack.

"All right. You live in the city. But surely you've been up in the mountains before now."

"Not very often." In truth, she'd been fascinated by the mountains when she'd first moved here. She'd made several excursions to the Canyon Preserve to view the hummingbirds in early May and she'd found few things more lovely than the sight of the cactus flowers and wild poppies in bloom, the spindly, green-barked paloverdes veiled in yellow blossoms. Even the woody sprays of ocotillos wearing their flame-shaped orange flowers and the homely prickly pear cacti with their coffee-cup-size peach-and-yellow flowers were breathtaking in the spring.

"How come?"

"How come what?"

"How come you haven't spent much time in these mountains? You were always curious and eager to explore the beaches. Why haven't you spent more time exploring the mountains?"

Because Herbert hadn't shared her fascination with the mountains or her desire to explore them. He'd been more inclined to spend time at the country club. "Because I haven't wanted to. I keep telling you I've changed, but you don't believe me."

"Let's just say I find it hard to believe you've changed that much. You were as fascinated as I was when we talked about traveling to different places and diving for treasure. Haven't you been at all curious about the Lost Dutchman's Mine?"

Of course, she'd been curious. She'd read all the stories about the Superstition Mountains and the Lost Dutchman's Gold Mine. One couldn't live in Arizona and not be aware of the tales that surrounded the area and were so much a part of its history. But not for the life of her would she admit to Jack just how curious she'd been. "You're the treasure hunter, Jack. Not me."

"So what made you choose Arizona? I always thought you'd end up settling in Florida. You loved the sand and surf. You and I even talked about living there someday."

"I grew bored with the beach."

"So you moved to the desert?"

"I moved to Mesa because I liked the city and the people here."

From the expression on his face, Lorelei doubted that he believed her. The last thing she wanted him to know was that she'd chosen the desert because anywhere near water reminded her too much of him. "Is the generator working now?" she asked, eager to change the subject.

"Should be. Come on. Let's go see." He slipped an arm around her shoulder, and Lorelei promptly removed it. She fell into step beside him as he started toward the front of the cabin. "I'll get the lights on and bring the stuff in that we'll need for tonight. Can you handle your suitcase or do want me to get it for you?"

"I can handle it."

A few minutes later Jack had the cabin unlocked, and a soft, welcoming light glowed from the windows. Lorelei followed him up the steps. He took her suitcase from her and set it inside the door, then he turned to face her. His gaze slid over her like melted butter on hot popcorn before coming back up to meet her eyes.

Lorelei's pulse picked up speed as she recognized that look. It was the way he'd looked at her ten years ago when he'd met her that first time on the beach. It was the way he'd looked at her two weeks ago when he'd seen her again. It was the way he was looking at her now—like a man who'd been wandering through a desert without water for days and she was a cool mountain stream that he could barely wait to taste.

He wanted her.

She didn't want to feel that answering flicker of fire in her belly. She didn't want to feel that tug of desire for him, but she did.

"Since this is supposed to be our wedding night," he said, desire heating his blue eyes, "why don't I carry you over the threshold?"

"Get out of my way, Storm," she said coolly despite the fact that the blood was spinning in her veins. Pushing past him, she hurried inside the cabin and came to a dead stop.

The first thing that hit her, besides the fact that it was every bit as hot inside the cabin as it had been outside, was the size. The place was small, even by the standards of a woman who'd grown up sharing a room with two sisters. Too small, Lorelei decided. And much too cozy.

A Navajo rug stretched across the floor, providing a splash of color against the dark wooden planks. A stone fireplace dominated the room. Lorelei could imagine fires blazing in the hearth on cold winter nights and lovers snuggled up together in front of it.

She shifted her attention from that dangerous line of

thinking and scanned the rest of the room. A cluster of willowy cattails and dried stalks rose majestically from the mouth of a tall Native pot painted in splashes of red, green and yellow. Thick vanilla-and-sage-colored cushions dotted a large, comfortable-looking couch that was positioned on the opposite wall and took up a good portion of the room. A small kitchen area with a hot plate, sink, a table and two chairs occupied the rest of the space. A closed door led to what was evidently the bedroom. Considering her body's traitorous response to Jack earlier, Lorelei paled at the thought of the two of them sharing such close quarters—even for only a night.

"Dinner has arrived," Jack said, carrying in a stack of take-out containers. He kicked the door shut behind him and strode across the room to set the containers on the table. "There's no oven to reheat any of this stuff, but the containers are still warm. I suggest we go ahead and eat now while it's still relatively hot. Afterward we can get situated for the night."

If she hadn't already been warm, just thinking of spending the night here with Jack was enough to make her palms grow damp. "I'm not sure I could eat anything hot in this heat anyway."

"I turned on the window unit. It should start cooling off in here in a few minutes."

"What about tomorrow? I'm assuming from that tent I saw strapped to the truck, we're not staying in any hotels while we look for your treasure."

"Our treasure," he corrected. "It won't be too bad. And once we get higher in the mountains, it'll be cooler at night. What'll you have to drink? We've got canned soda, tea and bottled water."

"Water. Please."

Jack twisted off the bottle top and handed it to her. "Thanks."

"Isabel said she keeps a few dishes here if you want a glass."

"The bottle's fine." She took a long sip and sighed as the cool liquid slid down her throat.

Jack took the seat opposite her and drank from his own bottle of water. Alone in the small cabin without the jostling of the truck to distract her, Lorelei was very much aware of him. She watched in fascination as the muscles in his throat worked while he downed nearly half of the bottle's contents. Her gaze drifted to the opening of his denim shirt and the generous dusting of dark hair on skin bronzed by years in the sun. She couldn't help but remember lying naked against that chest, feeling the heat of his body next to her own.

"I thought you were hungry."

Lorelei blinked at the sound of Jack's voice. *Sweet mercy, I must be out of my mind. Why else am I sitting here in the middle of nowhere ogling Jack Storm and remembering the two of us making love?* "I am," she said, trying to banish the images from her thoughts. She popped open the lid on her dinner. The scent of burgers and chili permeated the air. Tearing open the packet of utensils Jack had given her, Lorelei used the plastic knife to slice her thick burger in half.

"Alberto makes a great burger," Jack told her between bites. "He'd tell you so himself, if he were here. Personally I think his chili's better. Go ahead and try it."

She did try it and even managed to eat a few bites of her burger while Jack continued the one-sided conversation.

"Remember the burgers we used to get at that little place in Fort Walton?"

"Cash's."

"Yeah. That's it. You were crazy about them, even insisted we pick some up to take with us down to our beach."

Our beach. The words sent a pang through her chest as sharp as a knife. The secluded stretch of sand and surf sandwiched between a series of dunes had been too small and far away from the resort and tourist areas to garner much traffic, particularly in early February. They had wandered upon the remote spot one day while out walking. They'd both been so caught up in Jack's tales of the faraway places he planned to visit, all the treasures he planned to find, that neither of them had realized just how far from the beaten path they'd strayed.

Afterward it had become "their beach." The place where they went to be alone together. The place where they planned and dreamed about the future. The place where he'd first told her he loved her, had asked her to marry him. The place where they'd first made love.

"I'll never forget you insisting we have a moonlight picnic." He paused. His eyes skimmed her face. "That was the first time I'd ever been on a picnic."

Lorelei sensed a loneliness, a hunger in him, that made her want to reach out. She forced herself to turn away.

"I haven't been on another picnic or walked on a beach in the moonlight since that last time we were there," he told her, his voice sounding raw, almost hoarse.

Lorelei looked up. The air conditioner buzzed in the background, shooting out blasts of cool air. But the air that stretched between them seemed to have grown thicker, charged with some invisible energy that was every bit as oppressive as the triple-digit heat had been. And with the tension, Lorelei felt the unwanted hum of desire stirring inside her.

"As long as I live, I don't think I'll ever forget the way you looked that night. You were wearing white shorts and a pale green T-shirt with a matching ribbon in your hair."

At the sound of his voice, soft and seductive, the longing in his eyes as he looked at her, Lorelei stopped pretending to eat. She put down her burger and simply stared at Jack. And found herself following him back into the past. Back to that summer ten years ago when they'd been alone on the beach...

"See? Didn't I tell you this was the perfect place for a picnic?" Lorelei asked as she finished the last of her hamburger and licked the mustard from her fingertips.

"Yes. And you were right, as usual." Jack caught her hand and stroked his tongue along the length of her fingers. A shudder went through Lorelei at the exquisite feel of his mouth and tongue moving across her flesh. She felt excited. Alive. Happy. And in love.

"You really are beautiful."

"So are you." Feeling bold, she captured his wrist. She could feel the wild beat of his pulse and knew she should stop. Instead, she held on and pulled him down to where she had stretched out across the blanket. "Kiss me."

Lowering his head, he brushed his mouth back and forth against hers. "Sweet. So sweet. I love you," he murmured.

Lorelei's heart soared at his words. She cupped his face in her hands. "And I love you."

"Always?" he asked, his voice a deep rumble. "Will you always love me?"

"Always," she promised, then pulled his mouth back to hers.

He slid his tongue along the seam of her lips, leaving a flame of desire wherever he touched. Lorelei felt the heat pool like warm honey between her thighs. The rhythmic sound of the surf rushing against the shore faded away as her heart moved from a trot to a full gallop in her chest. She opened her mouth to him, wanting more of the fire, more of the heat that was a part of Jack.

Jack tangled his hands in her hair, holding her prisoner, before dipping his head again and taking what she offered. He took. He gave. Then he took some more. The world slipped away. Her entire being centered around the feel of Jack's mouth, his wondrous mouth mating, fusing with hers.

He pressed his body against hers, and she could hear the harsh sounds he made deep in his throat, feel the rigid bulge in his pants pushing against her thigh. A thrill of pleasure and need shot through her.

He had kissed her before. Many times, in fact. But never like this. Never had any of his kisses tasted so dangerous, so wild, so desperate. They called to some dangerous, wild need inside her. Mimicking his movements, she returned his kiss, testing him, tasting him with her mouth, with her tongue. She curled her fingers into his hair, wanting him to be even closer.

Jack's fingers dug into her hips, made a frenzied journey up to her waist. He kneaded and stroked as he continued to taste her. Lorelei feasted on his mouth as he feasted on hers. Groaning, he slipped his hand beneath the hem of her T-shirt, inched his way up her stomach, along her rib cage, to her breasts. His hands and body went still when he discovered she hadn't bothered to wear a bra.

Her breasts were already achy and taut for the feel of his hands. She arched her back, wanting him to touch her, needing to feel his hands on her. She didn't realize until it was too late that she had said the words aloud.

Jack groaned again, then closed his fingers around her breasts and deepened the kiss.

Lorelei nearly went crazy at the erotic feel of his callused palms caressing her bare flesh. Never could she have imagined that lovemaking would be like this—so wild, so wonderful. But only with him. Only with Jack. She could feel his excitement, knew that they'd gone way past the boundaries she'd set for them. Aching for more, she eased her shaky hand between their bodies, moved it lower to stroke his hardness through his slacks.

Jack tore his mouth free and reared back his head. He sucked in air as though he'd just run a ten-mile marathon. His eyes blazed with a blue fire that should have frightened her. It excited her instead. "Oh, Lorelei. Sweetheart, I'm sorry. I didn't mean to let things go so far."

Since she was having a little difficulty breathing herself, it took a moment before she could tell him, "It's okay, Jack. Really." But it wasn't okay. Not anywhere near okay. She ached everywhere—her mouth, her breasts, between her thighs. She wanted him to kiss her again, touch her again. They loved one another. What could be so wrong about making love if two people loved one another?

Jack dragged a hand through his hair. "I'd better take you home." His voice sounded rusty, winded. "It's getting late."

"It's not that late. I don't want to go home, Jack. I want you to kiss me again." She swallowed. "I want you to touch me again."

A shaft of moonlight fell across his face. His black hair curled at his collar and bore the wrath of her restless fingers. Desire had darkened his eyes to a blue black. With his jaw clenched, his mouth unsmiling, he looked every inch the dangerous pirate.

"That's not such a good idea right now, sweetheart. If I kiss you again, I'm not going to want to stop and I know how you feel about sex before marriage."

She reached for his hand and pulled him down to her. "In my heart, I'm already married to you. Love me, Jack. Love me."

"Lorelei? Lorelei?"

Hearing her name, Lorelei tore her thoughts from the past. She blinked. Jack was sitting across the table staring at her. Another frown creased his forehead. His eyes were clouded with concern. "You okay? Something wrong with your dinner?"

She looked down at the hamburger she still held in her hands and placed it back in the container. "The food's fine. I guess I'm just more tired than I realized." She needed to get away from him, to reel in her feelings before she did something stupid. "I don't suppose it would do me any good to ask you again to give up on this crazy idea of yours and take me back to Mesa, would it?"

"No."

"Then I think I'll just go on to bed." Lorelei pushed her chair back from the table and stood. Picking up the remains of her dinner, she dumped it in the trash can and started toward the door that led to the bedroom. The sooner she put some distance between her and Jack the better, she decided.

"Uh, Lorelei. There's something we have to talk about first."

"Let's wait until morning, Jack. I'm really beat."

"I'm afraid it can't wait."

"All right," she said, turning to look at him. "What is it?"

"There's only one bed."

Four

"Then I guess *you'll* have to take the couch," Lorelei told him as she moved toward the closed door.

"Lorelei."

"What?" she snapped, turning back to face him.

"The couch *is* the bed."

Her gaze darted to the couch and then back to him. "But I thought..." She pushed open the door that she'd obviously thought was the bedroom and discovered the bathroom and a closet instead. She whipped back around to face him. Her cheeks were flushed with anger, and she looked spitting mad. "You planned this," she accused.

"I didn't."

"I don't believe you."

"Tough," Jack countered, his own temper fraying a bit. "It's the truth. I swear it. I hadn't planned on us spending the night here. I thought we'd be camping out in the mountains by now." He shoved his hand through his hair. "If you hadn't been so stubborn and had agreed to talk to me when I asked you—"

"*What?*" She marched over to him, fury flashing in her brown eyes. "You're saying it's *my* fault that we're stuck here? You were the one who kidnapped me from my wedding, remember?"

Jack flushed at the truth of her accusation. "I didn't have much choice, did I? You refused to talk to me, to even give me a chance to explain," he said defensively. He knew he wasn't being completely fair. But he simply couldn't lose her again—not when he'd just found her. "I did what I had to do, Lorelei. I couldn't let you marry Herbert—at least not without trying to convince you that you were making a mistake."

"The only mistake I made was ever agreeing to marry you in the first place."

Jack winced at the verbal blow, feeling as though he'd just been socked in the gut. He gritted his teeth. "At least when you agreed to marry *me* it was because you loved me and not because we shared similar tastes in books."

Color rushed up her cheeks. "You don't know anything about what Herbert and I feel for one another."

"I know you don't feel passion." It had been one of the things that had given him hope. If he'd sensed Lorelei loved Herbert, his conscience wouldn't have allowed him to kidnap her as he had. But there had been no fire between the pair. Not the way it had been with them. The two of them had nearly burned one another up with the chemistry that had blazed between them. And when he'd kissed her again that day in the bookstore, the fire between them was just as hot, just as intense. No, he wasn't wrong. Lorelei didn't love her fiancé, no matter what she said. The question was could she love him again? "There was passion between us ten years ago, and whether you want to admit it or not, it's still there. And during the next ten days, I intend to prove it."

"Ten days! You can't be serious."

Guilt zipped through him at her horrified expression. Just as quickly, he shoved it aside. "Oh, I assure you, I am serious. I've never been more serious about anything in my life. I want ten days, Lorelei—one day for each year that I've lost with you."

"To do what? Search for some stupid gold mine?"

"Finding the mine isn't the only thing I want. I want a chance to try to change your mind about me, about us."

"There is no *us*."

"That's what we're going to find out."

She narrowed her eyes. "And after ten days you'll take me back to Mesa?"

"If that's what you still want. If I can't convince you that we belong together in that time, then I'll bring you back to Herbert and get out of your life for good." But just the thought of doing that left a sick feeling in his belly.

"I don't need ten days, Jack. I can tell you right now, I'm not going to change my mind."

"That's what we're both going to find out."

She hiked up her chin. "What if I refuse to go with you?"

"You don't have any choice," he said firmly. He was right about them being together. He was sure of it—just as he had been sure that the map he had in his possession was the "real" map, the one that would lead them to the Dutchman's treasure. The treasure and Lorelei. The two were connected—at least for him. Somehow he knew he was meant to find them both. "Either you come with me willingly or I'll carry you if I have to. In fact, that might not be such a bad idea," he said, giving her a smile that he hoped would coax her into a better mood. "I've always liked the feel of you in my arms."

The remark earned him another glare. Snatching up her bag, she shoved open the bathroom door.

"You go ahead and take the bathroom first while I clean

up in here," Jack said, and winced when she slammed the door in his face. Sighing, he let out a deep breath. While the battle wasn't over by any means and he didn't trust her not to try to run away again, at least she wasn't still fighting him over the issue of the bed.

With that in mind, Jack started tidying up the kitchen. Once everything was in order, he switched off the light and set about opening the sofa.

By the time he had the sheets on and the covers turned down, Lorelei still hadn't emerged from the bathroom. The water had shut off ages ago, so he knew she wasn't still in the shower. Suddenly he wondered if the little fool had tried to take off again. He'd spotted the window from outside the cabin when he'd checked the generator out back earlier. The thing had looked too small for her to fit through, and surely she wasn't crazy enough to try escaping in the dark. But then, he wouldn't put anything past Lorelei. Despite her insistence that she was an adult now and no longer given to what she considered juvenile escapades such as treasure hunting, there was still an adventuress and a risk taker in Lorelei even if she was well hidden. "Lorelei? You okay in there?"

"No. I am not okay," she said, and judging from the tone of her voice she was plenty ticked off.

"What's the problem?"

The door opened with a jerk, and steam billowed out, along with a whiff of some sweet, seductive scent that had him thinking of soft skin and hot sex. His body responded instantly.

"The problem is that the only thing my sister packed for me to sleep in is *this*."

A whisper of black silk hit him in the face. Jack caught it before it fell to the floor. He looked down at the sheer wisp of silk he held in his hands and decided it would provide about as much coverage as a piece of plastic wrap.

"Well? Aren't you going to say something?" she demanded.

Jack held up the gown, looking first at it and then at her. An image of Lorelei wearing it raced through his thoughts, and he nearly groaned aloud. His blood heated; his body began to throb.

"Jack!"

"I don't mind you sleeping in it, if you don't," he finally managed to say, not bothering to hide his grin.

Lorelei made an exasperated sound and snatched it from his fingers. "You'll have to lend me one of your shirts."

Since she looked angry enough to chew nails, Jack decided not to argue. Besides, he told himself, sleeping tonight was going to be difficult enough without thinking of Lorelei lying in bed next to him wearing only that scrap of silk. He went over to his backpack, rummaged through it and pulled out a rust-and-black-checkered shirt. He handed it to Lorelei.

Grabbing it and the nightgown, she marched back into the bathroom and slammed the door shut behind her.

When Lorelei emerged from the bathroom a few minutes later, Jack wasn't sure that his shirt would prove any less dangerous to his peace of mind than the flimsy nightgown. In fact, he thought as he stared at her, it might even be worse. While the little black number had left nothing to the imagination, Lorelei in his shirt left far too much for him to imagine—and remember. Fawn-colored hair surrounded a heart-shaped face with a made-for-kissing mouth and eyes the color of burned sugar. Soft skin the shade of cream extended down a long, graceful neck that disappeared beneath the primly buttoned collar. The shirt gently flowed over her full breasts, skimmed along her narrow waist and curved rounded hips before coming to a halt at the top of a pair of smooth, slender thighs.

Desire slammed through him at the speed of a missile, and Jack wondered how in the world he had managed to live the past ten years without making love to Lorelei, when right now he wasn't sure he would be able to make it through even one night. All he could think about was opening those buttons one by one, peeling that shirt off of her, lowering his mouth to first one breast and then the other, taking the tip between his teeth…

"I think you should sleep in the truck."

Jack jerked his thoughts back to the present and stared at Lorelei, standing before him with her hands perched on her hips, a militant expression on her face. "What?"

"I said, I think you should sleep in the truck," she repeated, pushing her chin up another notch.

So much for his X-rated thoughts, Jack decided. "Forget it. I'm not sleeping in any damn truck. That's a king-size bed, and there's room enough in it for both of us."

"Then I'll sleep in the truck," she countered.

"That's not an option."

"It's an option if I say it is! There's no way I'm going to get in that bed with you, Jack Storm."

He gave her a thin smile. "What's the matter, sweetheart? Don't trust yourself to keep your hands off of me?" he asked, knowing as he said it that the remark would set her off.

"Don't you wish."

"Oh, yeah. I wish, all right. You have no idea just how much wishing I do where you're concerned." And it was true. He wished he could go back to that time ten years ago. If he could, if he had it to do all over again, he'd pass on the dive that day no matter how good the money might be. He would meet her at the justice of the peace's office and marry her just as they'd planned. His chest ached as he looked at her and thought of all that he'd lost by making the wrong choice that day. No, he didn't have the luxury of going back, but that didn't mean he couldn't fix things. The map had brought him to her again, and by kidnapping her he'd stolen a second chance. Somehow, this time he would make it work—for both of them.

With that thought in mind, Jack grabbed his gear and started for the bathroom. As he moved past her, he saw Lorelei's gaze stray to the table where he'd left the truck keys. He continued into the bathroom anyway. After turning on the shower, he counted down from twenty while he stripped off his clothes. When he reached number one, he wrapped a towel around his waist and eased open the door to the main room. Lorelei stood before the table, her hand hesitating over the truck keys. With the hum of the air conditioner and the running water to drown out the sound of his footsteps, Jack moved in behind her. "Thinking of taking a late-night cruise?"

Lorelei whirled around and barreled into his bare chest. He snagged the keys from her fingers. Her breasts rose and fell as she sucked in, then released a shocked breath. Even with the shirt between them, he could feel her tips harden at the contact. Her soft thighs brushed against his legs as she attempted to move. Jack's body responded immediately, his maleness pressing against her belly. Her eyes widened—with awareness and an answering heat that made Jack's throat go dry.

"I thought you went to shower," she said accusingly. She tried to step back, but with the table behind her, there was no place to go.

"I did, but then I thought it might be a good idea if I took these with me," he told her, holding up the keys. "Of course, you're more than welcome to join me in the shower and try to steal them again."

"Go soak your head, Storm," Lorelei retorted, and pushed her way past him.

When he exited the bathroom fifteen minutes later, he'd not only soaked his head but his entire body under a steady stream of cold water. It hadn't helped. He was just as hard, and aching for her just as much now as he had been when he'd stepped under the spray. It didn't seem to matter that his body was exhausted, that he'd had only four hours' sleep the night before because it had taken him that long to convince Desiree to help him. And once she had agreed, he'd had to move faster than a bloodhound on a hunt to get the supplies together and fine-tune his plans. Shanghaiing Lorelei at the church, battling with her all day while he'd itched to make love to her, had only added to the toll on his body.

Flipping off the light, Jack made his way to the bed. A ribbon of moonlight streamed through the window, bathing her sleeping form in its soft glow. She was curled up on the far corner of the bed with her back to him. Brown hair streaked with threads of gold spilled down her shoulders and fanned out onto the pillow. A sheet had been pulled up to cover her legs.

Jack eased his body into the bed, not wanting to disturb her. But the moment his head touched the pillow, he caught her scent. The smell of flowers—not your run-of-the-mill daisies or roses, but some sweet, perfumed bloom like honeysuckle, something every bit as intoxicating and sensual as the woman herself—wrapped itself around him.

Lorelei stirred beside him, the sheet slipping off her body to reveal a long, shapely leg. The all too familiar throbbing in his lower body started once more. Jack sighed. He stretched his arms up to cup them behind his head and stared up at the ceiling. He might as well prepare himself, he decided. It was going to be a long night.

Lorelei snuggled closer to the warmth and smiled, enjoying the feel of strong arms wrapped around her, the large hand possessively cupping her bottom.

The hand cupping her bottom?

Her eyes popped open, and she looked into Jack's sleeping face—a handsome, dark angel's face with chiseled cheekbones, charcoal black lashes and a poet's mouth. A mouth that was only a breath away from her own. Her heart seemed to leap to her throat.

Oh, Lord. How did I end up like this?

She squeezed her eyes closed a moment, recalling that she'd grown cold during the night and had burrowed toward the warm spot in the center of the bed. Evidently Jack had been the source of that warmth.

Opening her eyes, Lorelei kept her hand still where it rested on his chest. She moved her leg slightly, trying to ease it away from his. Jack shifted and managed to trap her leg more firmly between his.

Biting her bottom lip, Lorelei considered her situation. She didn't want him to wake up and find her like this. She stared at his face in slumber while trying to figure out what to do, noting the fine lines etched at the corners of his eyes that hadn't been there ten years ago. The scattered strands of silver in his dark hair and the faint scar at his left temple were also new. Dark stubble shadowed his jaw and chin and the strip of skin just above his upper lip. She looked at that mouth again—the mouth that had made her knees go weak with just a grin when she had been a girl of eighteen. A shudder went through her as she remembered the taste and feel of that mouth, hot and demanding, against her own yesterday.

Panic raced through her. She had to formulate some kind of plan to escape. No way would she be able to manage ten days with him in the mountains without him guessing the truth. It was bad enough that he'd been right about her still being attracted to him. She was. Despite her denials, she still had feelings for him—strong feelings that had somehow managed to survive even after he'd broken her heart. And he *had* broken her heart, shattered it into tiny little pieces. In fact, for a long time she'd been unsure if it would ever heal.

When he hadn't shown up that day, she'd been so hurt, too hurt to even speak to him when he did finally call. Then when the days ticked away and he hadn't called again or come to see her, she'd realized what a fool she'd been to trust Jack. She'd worried herself sick, wondering how to tell her parents the predicament she found herself in when she'd gone home—pregnant and jilted.

But she'd never had to tell them or anyone because then she'd lost the baby. Their baby—hers and Jack's. Lorelei squeezed her eyes shut as the pain washed over her again. It didn't matter that she'd only been six weeks along or that Jack hadn't even known she was pregnant. Silently she mocked herself as she remembered her decision not to tell him about the baby until after they were married because she'd wanted to be sure he was marrying her out of love—and not obligation. As it turned out, her worries had been for nothing. Because Jack hadn't married her at all. He'd simply chosen not to show up.

She'd sworn then that she'd never leave herself open to that kind of hurt again. She'd vowed never again to allow herself to love anyone the way she had loved Jack. And she'd succeeded.

Staring at his sun-darkened face, she recalled the shock of seeing him walk into the bookstore that day and sweep her into his arms to kiss her. She'd discovered then that she hadn't been as successful in banishing him from her heart as she had thought. Jack Storm was every bit as dangerous to her now as he had been ten years ago. She couldn't, wouldn't leave herself open to the risk of loving him again. Ten days in the mountains with him? No way. It was too great a risk.

His heart beat evenly beneath her palm. From the steady rise and fall of his chest, he was obviously sound asleep. He must have finally gone down out of exhaustion, Lorelei decided, recalling how he'd tossed and turned for hours last night. Twice she'd awakened during the night and discovered he'd left the bed and gone outside. And now he was dead to the world. If she were going to run away, now was the time to do it.

With that thought in mind, slowly she attempted to untangle her leg from between his. Triumph surged through her when she managed to do so without waking Jack. Gingerly she removed her hand from his chest and managed to press her back against the mattress. Taking care not to move too quickly, Lorelei turned over onto her side so that she was facing away from him. She lifted the hand that hovered near her shoulder, placing it gently on his own leg. Jack shifted and the hand came back, this time to rest on her hip.

Lorelei didn't move for long seconds, waiting for his breathing to grow even again and for the hand to stop kneading her hip. When he seemed to have settled back into sleep, she lifted his hand and removed it from her hip.

It came back almost immediately to cup her breast.

Lorelei sucked in her breath. She squeezed her eyes shut as his fingers, taking advantage of the buttons that had come open during the night, moved in lazy circles around the tip of her nipple. His touch was gentle, as soft as a whisper, but a trail of fire burned wherever he touched her. Liquid heat flowed through her and pooled between her thighs.

Frantic, Lorelei caught his wrist to stop the waves of pleasure and torture he was creating inside her. Once again she removed his hand from her body and started to edge away.

Jack's hand came around her again and clamped onto her breast once more. Then he pulled her bottom against his lower body—his very aroused lower body.

Lorelei froze. Fury exploded through her. Breaking free of his arms, she whipped around and stared into Jack's laughing blue eyes.

"Morning, beautiful," he said, his mouth splitting into

that quick, mischievous grin before dipping to brush his lips against hers.

"You...you big fake!" She scrambled off the bed. Glaring at him, she said, "Of all the lousy tricks. I thought you were asleep!"

"I was asleep. But then I woke up and found you lying next to me, in my arms, no less. I thought for sure I'd died during the night and had gone to heaven," he said, smiling. He patted the bed. "If you'll come back here and snuggle me again, I'm more than willing to try to go back to sleep."

Lorelei threw a pillow at him, smacking him in the chest. "I was trying not to wake you, you jerk. I knew you didn't sleep well last night."

"Hey, don't blame me. My difficulty sleeping was entirely your fault."

"My fault?" she repeated, astonished by the accusation.

"Yes. Your fault. I couldn't stop thinking about the way you looked in my shirt." His eyes slid over her like a caress, and the laughter slowly gave way to heat.

An answering heat started in the pit of Lorelei's stomach at the way Jack was looking at her, tasting her with his eyes as he had once tasted her with his mouth. Her blood grew warm as he continued to devour her from the other side of the bed with nothing more than a look. Her breathing quickened. She felt like a rabbit trapped in the gaze of a starving wolf. Only she had nowhere to run for safety. She wasn't even sure she wanted to run to safety if it meant running away from Jack. She could feel the tips of her breasts tighten into buds and arch against the soft cotton shirt.

"Damn, but that shirt looks good on you," he said in a voice that had suddenly gone raw, husky as though it hadn't been used for a very long time. As though he was finding breathing as difficult as she was.

Wrestling to get a grip on her sanity before she did something foolish, Lorelei tore her gaze away from Jack and looked down. Two buttons on her shirt had come loose, revealing the tops of her breasts and her unmistakable reaction to him. Her eyes shot up, and she saw that his gaze was riveted to the front of the shirt. Color raced up her cheeks as she spun around and pulled the shirt together to rebutton it.

"Lorelei." He whispered her name with such longing, she had to force herself not to turn around and go into his arms. Then he was standing behind her, gripping her shoulders gently. He lifted the hair from the back of her neck, and she could feel the heat of his breath on her skin.

Don't. But the word stuck in her throat. She squeezed her eyes shut as he brushed a feather-light kiss across the base of her neck.

"I want you, Lorelei, and I know you want me."

"You're wrong," she said in a shaky breath, and knew that it was a lie. She did want him. Heaven help her, he could still make her body burn at his touch.

"No, I'm not. You know I'm not. Come back to bed, sweetheart. It's what we both want."

It was true. She knew it. She did want him and it would be so easy to give in to the sweet heat unfolding inside her and make love with Jack. His hands traveled down to her waist, kneaded the soft flesh. Her legs felt as if they'd turned to butter, and she could feel herself weakening as that clever mouth of his continued to taste the tender spot at the base of her neck.

He tugged her body closer, pressing her bottom against him. Lorelei swallowed. There was no mistaking that he was fully awake now.

"Let me love you," he murmured, flicking the shell of her ear with his tongue.

She shuddered. Her blood swam.

And then he was turning her around to face him. "Look at me, Lorelei. Look at me."

With effort she opened her eyes to gaze up at him. She

stroked the stubble along his cheeks. Catching her fingers, he brought them to his lips. She felt herself sinking for a third time and started to move closer to him. "Jack." She reached up to touch his face.

Suddenly his eyes widened. His face paled beneath his tan, and he let out an ear-shattering yell.

Five

Thank heaven for spiders, Lorelei thought as she watched Jack give a wide berth to the corner where he'd seen the tarantula. If it hadn't been for him spying the hairy orange-and-black critter, she had no doubts that she would have succumbed to temptation and gone to bed with him.

And boy, what a mistake that would have been. She wasn't sure which would have proved more dangerous to her—being bitten by the tarantula or letting herself fall for Jack again. Too bad her allergic reaction to most insect and spider bites made the hairy little bugger potentially fatal to her. Otherwise, she might have considered trying to capture the nasty pest and using it as a weapon to coerce Jack into taking her back to Mesa.

Lorelei shut the lid on her suitcase and snapped the locks into place. A smile tugged at her lips as she recalled the look of outright terror that had crossed Jack's face—not to mention the volume of his "Oh my God's", "Hell's" and "Look out's" before he'd tossed her onto the bed and scrambled in behind her. His quick change of mood had certainly brought her back to her senses. Still, in all those months she'd known him, loved him, even planned to marry him years ago, she'd never discovered that he had a fear of spiders. In truth, Jack had always seemed so reckless and daring, so full of self-confidence that she hadn't thought he was afraid of anything.

"You about ready?" Jack asked, eyeing the corner near the window where the spider had scooted to before slipping through a cracked floorboard to go outside.

"I'm ready," she said, unable to hold back a chuckle at his skittish glance to the corner again.

"It's not funny, Lorelei," he said as he took the suitcase from her.

"Oh, but it is."

A flush crawled up his neck and face as he stomped out of the cabin and locked the door behind them. Marching over to the Explorer, he dumped her suitcase in the back of the truck.

"Who would have thought that big, macho Jack Storm, the man who's braved the world in his quest for buried treasure, would be afraid of a teeny-weeny little spider."

He slammed the tailgate shut. "It wasn't a little spider. It was huge."

"If you say so," she said with a grin. Climbing into the front seat, she buckled her seat belt while Jack placed the key to the cabin beneath a potted cactus on the porch. To be fair, the thing had been large—almost the size of her fist. And if she'd seen the thing first, she would have been scared silly, too. As it was, she'd only caught a fleeting glimpse of orange and black scooting beneath the floorboard because she'd been too busy sinking in the quicksand of Jack's kisses. Once her breathing had returned to normal, the spider was long gone, leaving a wide-eyed, pale-faced Jack behind. She grinned again. Even now she couldn't shake the memory of Jack abandoning his attempt to seduce her—an attempt that was darn near successful—for the simple reason that he was afraid of a spider.

"It *was* huge," he insisted once more before stomping around to the driver's side of the truck and getting in. Still scowling, he strapped himself into the seat and shot her a defiant look. "And it was also dangerous. Suppose the thing had bitten one of us? A tarantula's bite can be extremely painful, and the nearest hospital is over in Apache Junction."

"I know." It was true. One of the first rules she'd learned when she'd moved to Arizona and made her first trip into the desert was that despite their appearance, the geckos and Gila monsters were not especially dangerous. And while the bite of a tarantula was painful, it wasn't deadly—at least not to most people. But given her violent reaction the two times she'd been bitten by an insect—first a bee as a child and later a caterpillar in her garden—chances were the tarantula would prove to be just as lethal. That's why she'd done her best to make sure they didn't cross one another's paths.

Or at least they hadn't crossed paths until Jack had kidnapped her. With that thought in mind, she said, "You know, Jack, you might want to rethink this plan of yours that has us traipsing through the mountains looking for some fictitious gold mine."

"The Dutchman's Mine isn't fictitious. It exists. And we're going to find it," he said firmly as he started the engine.

"I've heard these mountains are full of spiders—all kinds."

"Then I guess we'll have to make sure that we give them a wide berth."

"Just so I'm prepared, is there anything else you're afraid of that I should know about? You know, things like lizards? Maybe snakes?" In truth, just the thought of either creature made her want to shiver.

"Nope. In fact," he said, shooting her a challenging grin, "if we find ourselves running short on supplies, snake can be quite a tasty meal."

Lorelei did shiver at that thought. "I'll take your word for it," she said stiffly, and sat back in her seat. "The idea of eating a snake, let alone running into one, has about as much appeal for me as that tarantula did for you."

Jack turned the wheels of the Explorer onto the road, setting dirt and bits of gravel spitting out from beneath the tires. "Then I guess you're going to have to trust me to protect you from all those snakes."

"And who's going to protect you from the spiders?" she countered quickly, while wondering who was going to protect her from him.

His smile widened. "I guess I'll just have to trust you to protect me."

"I wouldn't count on that if I were you."

"Come on, sweetheart. Admit it. You still have feelings for me."

"How does *contempt* sound?" she challenged.

It didn't faze him. "If you didn't care about me or really wanted to leave, you would have tried to make a run for it last night while I was asleep. Lord knows I was dead to the world."

"Don't delude yourself, Storm. *You* took the truck keys, remember?"

"You could have tried to steal them again."

The thought had crossed her mind. More than crossed it. She had actually considered it and would have done so—except that Jack had tucked the keys into his pocket and she hadn't wanted to risk trying to get them from his pants with him still in them. Not that she would admit it. "I decided it would be foolish to risk my neck trying to find my way down the mountain in the dark."

"Then I guess I don't have to worry about you trying to murder me in my sleep and stealing the truck, then."

"Don't push your luck, Jack. I still might kill you. Keep this up, and I just might start reconsidering whether or not murdering you is worth a stretch in prison."

"Now, is that any way to talk to the man you're going to marry?"

"Jack," she said, practically growling his name.

He chuckled. "Face it, Lorelei. You're still as much in love with me as I am with you."

His cocky remark infuriated her. In part because she was very much afraid that it might be true. How else did she explain that achy feeling in her chest when she thought of him? Or the way he could make her blood spin with just a look? But she knew all too well the danger of loving Jack Storm. While he might love her as he said, it would never be enough. She would always come in second to his need for adventure. Hadn't he proved that to her once already? "You really do fantasize, don't you?"

"All the time—especially about you and me, about us getting married."

She cursed her treacherous pulse as it picked up speed. "The only man I plan to marry is Herbert."

Jack laughed again. "It's a good thing your sister's the actress, Lorelei. Because you're a lousy liar. Or did you forget *I* was on the receiving end of that kiss last night?" He swerved to miss a hole in the road and sent dust flying up in front of the truck and the two of them jostling in their seats.

"Don't kid yourself," he said, the laughter fading from his lips. "If that little hairy monster hadn't made an appearance this morning when he did and given you a chance to think instead of feel, you and I both know we'd be back in the cabin right now with me buried deep inside you and you calling out *my* name." He cut her a glance that was as dark and dangerous as his voice. "You can bet the next time I've got you in my arms all hot and clinging, an army of spiders won't be able to stop us from seeing it through."

A shiver of excitement skimmed through her body. Damn him, Lorelei thought, hating the tingle of anticipation his words had set off. "There isn't going to be a next time," she told him, and meant it. "Because the first chance I get, I'm out of here."

"Then I guess I'll just have to make sure you don't get another chance."

And she didn't have a chance over the next few hours as Jack sent the Explorer twisting through a forest of mesquite and saguaro trees on what seemed to be an endless, teeth-rattling, dusty dirt road. When he finally brought the truck to a stop and suggested they stretch their legs, Lorelei was more than willing.

But the minute she stepped out of the truck and its air-conditioned cab, the heat smacked her in the face like a load of dry sand and nearly stole her breath away.

"Feel up to a little hike?" Jack asked.

"And if I don't?" she countered, feeling ornery and wondering why the heat didn't seem to bother Jack.

He shrugged. "Then we can eat lunch in the truck. But you should know, there's a nice spot just up through those trees over there that I think you'll like. It'd be a shame for you to miss seeing it just to spite me."

Lord, was she so transparent? "All right," she told him. "I need to stretch my legs anyway."

Jack winked at her. "That's my girl."

Her crazy pulse did a fast Irish jig, and she looked away from him and out to the vast canyon that stretched below them. The greenish black rock formations rose up like stony fingers stretching toward a faded blue sky that appeared to be almost bleached white from the sun. Lorelei remembered reading the stories of how the Pima Indians had feared the mountains and how their superstitions had led to the mountains' name.

"Hey, city girl, you coming?"

Lorelei turned back to Jack, who had grabbed a knapsack from the truck and hooked a canteen to his belt. He stopped and fished out a tube of sunscreen. "You might want to put some of this on so you don't burn," he said, offering it to her. "I know how much you hate those cute little freckles popping up on your nose."

She reached for the sunblock, but Jack didn't release it. Her eyes shot up to meet his. That mischievous grin curved his lips as his gaze slipped from her face, down over her white cotton blouse to the legs exposed by her olive shorts. Slowly he journeyed up again to meet her eyes. "Better yet, why don't I put it on for you?"

Lorelei snatched the tube from his hand and turned her back to him. She sat down on a rock and quickly slathered some of the lotion on her arms, her legs and across the tip of her nose, wishing all the while that she could blame the fevered tingling of her skin on the heat of the sun. She knew that she couldn't—not when Jack was the cause.

Irritated with herself, she stood. "Well, are you going to show me whatever it is you've found so we can eat lunch, or do you plan to spend the rest of the day standing in there ogling me like some teenager with a girlie magazine?"

Jack hesitated. His eyes slid over her again, and he rubbed his jaw as though he were considering the option.

"Jack!"

"All right," he said, smiling. "Come on."

Reluctantly taking his hand, Lorelei followed him into the canyon through a cleft in the sheer mountain wall. Jack led her through rocky lower terrain past more saguaros and tree chollas with nasty barbed spines. As they ascended, she forgot all about eating as she stared at the sight before her. A wind-smoothed ridge seemed to wave before them like a yellow-and-mauve pennant. Stony fingers easily measuring fifty feet and higher lined the upper canyon, creating maze after maze of passages. A part of her wanted to rush over and explore the windowlike openings of the maze and discover where each of them led.

"Impressive, isn't it?" Jack asked as he ushered her beneath a rock cliff to sit down. He began unpacking their lunch.

"Yes," Lorelei agreed, accepting the summer sausage, bread and cheese he handed her. "I bet it's spectacular during the springtime." She could easily imagine the mesas covered in tall grass with the spikes of desert spoon flowers waving in the wind.

"We'll have to come back in the spring and see for ourselves."

Talk of the future jerked Lorelei back to the present and to her predicament. She couldn't afford to allow herself to get caught up in the seductive web Jack spun so skillfully. To do so would prove every bit as painful as the tarantula's bite. Maybe even more so, judging by what happened the last time she'd become involved with him.

No, instead of allowing herself to be charmed by him, she had to plan her escape.

Jack angled another glance at Lorelei out of the corner of his eye. He could almost see the wheels turning as she sat beside him in silence, watching, studying, looking back at the road they'd traveled.

What I wouldn't give to be able to crawl inside that head of hers for five minutes. Did she really think he didn't know she was going to try to run away again? Did she really think he'd let her?

He frowned. The trail had become less easy to negotiate as the hours ticked by and they'd climbed deeper into the mountains. The mixture of gravel and dirt gave way to dust, and the road had grown more shallow. Hell, he was an experienced tracker and even *he* wouldn't attempt to travel this road in the dark. But knowing the stubborn streak in Lorelei, he doubted that a little thing like darkness would deter her. And judging by the way the sun had been playing along the western rim of the mountain, casting them in and out of shadow for the past hour, it wouldn't be long before the road clearly visible in daylight transformed into a barely discernible strip that became ten times more dangerous to maneuver in the inky blackness of night.

Thirty minutes later, when the bleached blue sky started to give way to the rising moon, Jack pulled the truck to a stop and into a clearing at the side of the road. "I think we'll call it a day and set up camp here for the night."

Cutting off the engine, he left the keys in the ignition and exited the truck. He noted Lorelei's gaze shift to the keys as he moved to the rear of the vehicle and began unloading their gear. "I'll go ahead and pitch the tent. There's some food stuff in that bag over there," he said, pointing to the khaki-colored canvas. "Think you can put something together for us to eat?"

"Like what?"

"Doesn't matter to me. Whatever you decide on is fine. I'll eat just about anything," he said, noting the way her eyes darted once more to the truck keys. Walking around to the front of the truck, he snagged the keys from the ignition. "Almost forgot these," he said with a smile before slipping them into his pocket.

Lorelei tossed him a frosty look and exited the Explorer. "Afraid I'll steal the truck and leave you stranded here?"

"Would you?"

She hiked up her chin. "No," she replied, following him to the rear of the truck. "But not because I'd have any qualms about leaving you. I wouldn't."

"I didn't think so." Jack pulled out the tent and hefted it onto his shoulder.

"But as I've already told you, I'm not an idiot. I wouldn't be foolish enough to try to find my way down this mountain in the dark. I'd wait until morning."

"Then I guess I don't have to worry about handcuffing you to me tonight."

"Handcuffing me!"

"Actually I was planning to use a rope. But since you've told me you won't try to run off, I'll just forget about it." Amused by her shocked expression, he dropped a quick kiss across her open mouth. "In the meantime why don't you grab that backpack with the food and bring it down while I set up camp."

Turning away from a glaring Lorelei, he headed down the incline. His hiking boots shifted and grabbed on the rough surface as he made his way down to the clearing. Jack winced slightly when he heard the door to the Explorer slam, followed by her grumbling something about pig-headed pirates as she stomped on the path behind him.

Whistling, he went to work pitching the tent while Lorelei sorted through the food items. "How's dinner coming?" he asked, and earned himself another glare.

"The most appetizing thing here—and I use the word *appetizing* lightly—is canned beef stew."

"Stew's fine with me."

"I wasn't asking for your approval," she informed him as she unbagged utensils and tin plates. "Are we supposed to eat this stuff out of the can or heat it?"

Jack finished driving another stake for the tent and wiped his arm across his brow. "It's up to you. If you want it hot, there's a small camping stove in the truck you can heat it on, or if you want to gather up some sticks, I'll build us a fire and heat it on the portable grill. Or you can eat it cold. It's up to you."

Lorelei opted for hot, and by the time they sat down to eat, Jack was glad she had. As the sun sank, so had the temperature. The 110-plus-degree temperature that had made just walking seem like an aerobic exercise dipped to a somewhat chilly midsixties.

"Cold?" Jack asked as Lorelei rubbed her hands up and down her arms.

"A little." She edged closer to the fire he'd started and poured herself another cup of coffee.

"Enjoy it while you can. Once the sun comes up, the temperature's going to shoot back up, too."

Lorelei groaned. "I don't suppose it would do me any good to ask you one more time to give up this insane idea of yours to go looking for the mine. Would it?"

"Nope."

"Do you even know where you're going? Or were you just intending to drag me across the mountains for the next eight days?"

"I know where I'm going. Or at least the general area. Don't worry. It's not much farther. We should reach the area I plan to make our base camp tomorrow." Jack poked at the fire. "Once we set up camp, we'll need to go the rest of the way on foot."

Lorelei paused with the cup midway to her lips. "You mean we're going to leave the truck?"

He nodded. "The stretch of canyon we want isn't passable by truck. The truth is, we'll be lucky if there's even a road."

She set down the cup. In the glow of the firelight, her cognac-colored eyes reminded him of his first bottle of Remy St. Jacques. After years of small strikes and second-rate everything, he'd blown five hundred dollars on the granddaddy of cognacs. It had been a purchase he'd never regretted. Not only had the stuff tasted ten times better than the nickel-and-dime stuff he used to buy, but the color was richer, more vibrant, more potent.

Just like Lorelei.

"Jack, this is crazy. People have been searching for the Dutchman's Mine for more than a hundred years, and no one's ever found it."

"They didn't have the map. I do."

"There are dozens of maps. More than half the tourist shops in Arizona sell the blasted things."

"But my map's the *real* one. It's the one that Jacob Waltz gave to Julia Thomas when he was dying."

Lorelei frowned. "The bakery woman who supposedly took care of him when he was ill?"

"Yes," Jack replied, pleased that Lorelei knew some of the history.

"You mean to tell me we're on this wild-goose chase because you have a piece of paper with crazy scribbles on it that the Dutchman supposedly gave to a bakery woman?"

"He did give it to her," Jack said defensively. "She and the Dutchman were friends for years, and he was grateful to her for nursing him. He knew he was dying and would never be able to go back to his mine—that's why he drew her a map showing her where the mine was located. He wanted her to have it."

"Oh, Jack."

"It's true. And I have that map he gave her." To prove his point, Jack flipped open his backpack and removed the plastic bag that contained the worn, faded parchment. Moving next to Lorelei, he offered it to her for inspection. "Here. Take a look."

She looked at the crude drawing with its figures of mountains, cliffs and tunnels, then back up at him. She didn't believe it was genuine. He could see it in her eyes. And her doubts ate at him as nothing else could. Had he been wrong? Was he on a wild-goose chase as she claimed?

"Jack, everyone who's ever lived in or visited this area knows the tale of the Dutchman and his mine. Even if this map was authentic—"

"It *is* authentic," he told her with more conviction than he felt at the moment. It had to be authentic. He'd felt it in his gut. That's why he'd accepted it in lieu of cash in the high-stakes poker game. But where Lorelei was concerned, he'd been wrong before, he reminded himself. He'd been so sure she would be waiting for him when he got back from the boat that day.

"Jack, if the map is genuine, why didn't this Julia Thomas woman find the mine after the Dutchman gave this to her? Why hasn't anyone else ever found the mine since?"

"Because they weren't me. And they didn't have you for good luck. You're my luck, Lorelei." He caught a strand of gold-and-brown hair and curved it around his fingers. "Don't you see? The moment I saw you in that bookstore again, I knew this map was real. That this time I'd make the big strike. The map's what led me to you. And with you, I'll be able to find the mine."

"Don't." Lorelei turned her head when he would have kissed her. He caught the hitch in her voice, saw the flash of pain in her eyes. She shoved the map at him and stood.

"Lorelei."

She turned away from him. "Is that the real reason I'm here, Jack? Because you think I'm some kind of good-luck charm?"

There it was again in her voice—the hurt. He pushed the map aside and came to stand behind her. He closed his fingers around her shoulders and squeezed. A gust of wind raced through the campsite, setting the flames to dance. A lock of Lorelei's hair flickered across her face. The scent of smoke and Lorelei wrapped itself around him as he caught one fawn-colored strand of hair and tucked it behind her ear. Hope and desire made his heart pound. "You're here with me because I love you and I want a second chance."

"To do what? Break my heart again?"

Jack winced as her verbal arrow hit its mark. "I never meant to hurt you, Lorelei. It's the last thing I ever wanted to do."

"Then why did it take you ten years to come after me?" she demanded, whirling around to face him.

He met the anger and scorn in her eyes and knew he deserved them both. "I called—"

"Twice. You called me two times. And when I refused to speak to you because I was too angry and too hurt, you didn't even bother to call again. Or even come to see me."

"I couldn't. The boat was only in for three hours to get some equipment and was set to leave again. I came back the next month, when the dive was over, but you were already gone. You and your family had already left." He recalled his panic at discovering she'd left. "I wrote, hoping the letter would be forwarded to you."

"It was."

"But you never read it. You sent it back unopened."

"Do you blame me?"

"No," he said, his voice harsher than he'd intended. He didn't blame her. He blamed himself. Had blamed himself every time he thought of her and what he had lost. "Don't you think I know you had every right to be angry with me? To even hate me? That's why I decided not to come after you right away. I thought the best thing I could do was to give us both some time."

"I may have been crushed, Jack. But believe me, it didn't take me ten years to get over you."

"That's not what I meant."

"It didn't take me more than a few weeks to realize what a disastrous mistake we'd nearly made."

"It wouldn't have been a mistake, damn it."

"Then why has it taken you ten years to come after me?"

"Because I wanted..." He swallowed. He'd wanted to make a big strike first. To come to her a success, with something more to offer than a promise when he asked her to give him a second chance.

"Because you wanted what?"

"Because I wanted to be able to offer you more than just a dream and a promise."

"And what are you offering me now, Jack?"

Her words were as sharp as the tip of a saber and went straight to his heart. "If I'm right, I'll have the Dutchman's gold to offer you."

"I don't want it. I was never interested in money. I'm still not. I don't want any of the blasted gold."

"Tough," Jack told her, caging her face between his hands. "Because I'm going to find it and when I do, I'm going to give it to you. I swear it." He ran his thumb across her bottom lip and started to lower his head.

"Don't," she whispered, catching his wrists with her fingers.

"I have to." He brushed his lips across hers. "Because I love you. I've always loved you. I always will. Please, Lorelei, give us another chance."

For a moment he thought she was going to refuse, and his heart came to a stop. Then her eyes fluttered closed. Her body swayed toward him. Desire heated his blood, making his hands shake as he speared his fingers in her hair and murmured her name before he pulled her against him. He wanted to ravage that mouth, feed on her sweetness. Instead, he forced himself to kiss her slowly, gently. When she parted her lips, allowing him entry, Jack groaned and slid his tongue inside to dance with hers.

A wild animal cry sliced through the night, and Lorelei jerked her mouth free. "W-what was that?" she asked, digging her fingernails into his arms.

His body was as taut as a bowstring, and he drew in air, feeling as though he'd just run a marathon. "Probably some coyote's dinner."

Lorelei shuddered. "Thanks. I can't tell you how much comfort that is. It's bad enough that I probably won't be able to sleep a wink worrying about spiders and snakes getting in the tent. Now I can add the pleasant image of becoming some coyote's next meal."

Jack saw no reason not to take advantage of the fear that

had her clinging to him. He ran his hand up and down her spine and pulled her a bit closer. "There's nothing to be afraid of. The coyotes aren't going to bother us."

"How do you know? I've heard coyotes travel in packs. They even attack dogs bigger than they are. What's to stop them from coming after us?"

"They won't," he murmured soothingly as he kissed her on that sensitive spot just below her ear. "For one thing there's too many other creatures for them to feed on out there that would be easier prey." He moved to the side of her jaw. "For another the fire will keep them away."

"But what if...what if the fire goes out?"

Her voice had gone low and husky, whiskey rough and hot. Jack's body groaned. He was already rock hard and he hadn't done more than kiss her. "Then the coyote will have to get through me first because I don't intend to let you out of my arms tonight."

Lorelei pulled back slightly. Those brown eyes narrowed, glinted suspiciously. "What's that supposed to mean?"

"It means we'll be sharing the same tent." Jack grinned and attempted to ease her back into his arms. "And since you're afraid, we'll just go ahead and put our sleeping bags together."

Lorelei stiffened. Her gaze shifted to the tent and back to him. She pressed her hands against his chest, keeping him at arm's length. "Forget it, Jack. I'll take my chances with the coyotes."

Six

Lorelei swatted at something tickling her cheek. Between watching out for the coyotes and glaring at a peacefully sleeping Jack, she had lain awake for hours. Of course, listening to the steady hum of Jack's breathing less than two feet away from her hadn't helped. How was she supposed to be able to sleep with the man lying beside her half-naked and looking so darn sexy?

The pesky little insect brushed the corner of her mouth—only this time, instead of feeling like a butterfly, it felt distinctly like a man's lips. A man's lips? Lorelei opened her eyes and stared at Jack's grinning face.

"Morning, beautiful," he said, and promptly kissed her. "Time to get up."

"Go away," she told him, and closed her eyes. She'd never been a morning person and distrusted anyone who started the day off with bright eyes and a cheery smile.

"Nope." He kissed her again, this time allowing his lips to linger.

The seductive warmth of his mouth was just a little too tempting, and Lorelei felt an unwanted stirring in her body. Disturbed by her response, she shoved him away and turned over onto her side. She groaned as every muscle in her body screamed. Lord, but she hurt. Even muscles she hadn't been aware she owned were shrieking in protest from a night spent sleeping on the hard ground. "Whoever started the rumor that camp-outs were fun was a liar and a sadist," she muttered.

"Come on, sleepyhead. It wasn't that bad. I slept like a rock. Nothing like a night spent out under the stars, breathing in all that clean mountain air."

"Jack."

"Yeah."

"Go jump off a cliff."

"Didn't sleep well, did we?" he asked, laughter in his voice.

Lorelei answered with a growl and attempted to snuggle down into her bedroll, wanting only to go back to sleep.

"Don't worry. Tonight you'll sleep better."

"I'm not finished with last night yet," she informed him, and closed her eyes. "Besides, the sun's not even up yet."

Jack chuckled. "Sweetheart, I hate to tell you this, but that's not the moon glowing out there. The sun came up about half an hour ago. It's almost six o'clock."

"It can't be six o'clock. I just got to sleep a little while ago." She yawned. "Why don't you go look for buried treasure and wake me up in a couple of hours."

"Sorry. No can do. The Dutchman's treasure is what we're after, and if we're going to find it, we need to get on the road. So up and at 'em." When she didn't move, Jack smacked her bottom.

Lorelei whipped around to face him and bit back another groan as her muscles voiced their disapproval. Glaring at him, she said, "Watch your hands, Storm. Or I'll throw you off the cliff myself."

He cocked his head to the side as though giving her threat consideration. "Sounds like some kinky kind of foreplay to me. But, hey, I'm game if you are."

Lorelei squeezed her eyes shut and let out an exasperated breath. The man was impossible. So why did the flash of that devil smile of his and that crazy remark about foreplay make her pulse skitter?

"As tempting as the idea of making love to you is, I'm afraid we're going to have to wait. We really do need to get moving." He pressed a kiss to her mouth. "I've got the coffee ready. You go ahead and get dressed while I fix you some breakfast."

And then he was gone, leaving her with the taste of him on her lips. Lorelei touched her mouth. There was no point in lying to herself. Despite all that had passed between them, she still had feelings for Jack. Strong feelings. And how could she deny the chemistry between them when the least little touch or look from him had her breath hitching in her chest and her pulse going haywire? The pull between them was every bit as strong now as it had been ten years ago. Perhaps even more so, since now she knew how it would be between them.

Stop it, she commanded herself. Pushing back the cover of her sleeping bag, she stood and moved over to the backpack Jack had had her repack her clothes in. She pulled out a pair of shorts and a blouse. She couldn't give in to the sexual pull between them. To do so would be emotional suicide. After zipping up her shorts, she reached for her hiking boots and socks. She had to find a way to get off this mountain and away from him. Sitting down to lace up her boots, she spied Jack's wallet and keys next to his backpack.

Heart pounding, Lorelei cut a glance to the tent's opened flap. She could hear Jack whistling some tune as he worked over the campfire. She shifted her gaze back to the keys. If she was going to get away, now was the time to do it.

Another day alone with him, and no telling what fix her treacherous hormones would get her into. Quickly she came to her feet and moved over to where the keys lay.

"Lorelei!"

She jumped at the sound of Jack's voice and jerked her hand back. Her heartbeat roared like a drum in her chest as she whirled around to discover he wasn't behind her. "What?" she called out as she tried to slow her pounding heart.

"I'm starting your eggs. If you're not out here in two minutes flat, I'm coming in there to feed them to you myself. And when I finish feeding you, I'm going to crawl into that sleeping bag with you."

"I'm coming," she called out. Snatching up the keys, she shoved them into the pocket of her shorts and hurried outside.

"Thought that might get you moving," he said as she joined him in front of the campfire.

Ignoring his comment, she headed toward the spot she had claimed as a dinner seat last night. She was conscious of the weight of the truck keys in her pocket, where they seemed to burn against her hip, and thought that any minute Jack would demand she turn over the keys.

He didn't. Instead, his eyes moved over her like a caress, making her skin tingle and making her nervous in an entirely different way. No question about it, she decided as she sat down across from where he was finishing up the eggs, she'd done the right thing by stealing the keys. She had to escape before she did something really stupid—like let herself fall for him all over again.

"You feeling okay? You look flushed."

"Maybe it has something to do with the fact that I should be on my honeymoon now, not traipsing through the mountains with you looking for some gold mine."

Jack's lips thinned at the dig. She watched as guilty color rode up his neck and stained his face. Was it possible he actually felt bad about what he had done? "You mentioned something about coffee," she said, deciding it would be safer to change the subject.

He handed her a cup. She wrapped her fingers around it, glad to have something to hold on to so Jack wouldn't notice how badly her hands were shaking. She took a sip, even knowing as she did so that a boost of caffeine was the last thing her jumpy nerves needed.

"Here you go. Two eggs sunny-side up and bacon cooked crisp. Just the way you like it."

Lorelei stared at the food and wondered how in the world she was supposed to eat when her stomach was doing a Mexican hat dance. "What about you? Aren't you going to eat?"

"I already did about an hour ago. You go ahead. I'll have another cup of coffee and keep you company."

Great. How was she going to get to the truck if he was going to sit here and watch her? Lorelei managed to swallow a forkful of eggs and break off a bite of bacon while she debated what to do next. She was in relatively good shape, but she couldn't outrun him. The man was all solid muscle—muscles that she'd bet he hadn't earned in some fancy fitness center.

"You're awfully quiet this morning." He poured himself coffee and sat down across from her.

"I'm not prone to chattering first thing in the morning."

Jack grinned as he set down his cup. Lifting his arms, he folded them behind his head while he stretched out his legs and leaned against a rock. "No, you're not. I remember you didn't even like to hit the beach until noon."

"I never saw any point in freezing my bottom off by going swimming at dawn."

"Yeah. And I remember telling you I was more than willing to keep that cute little bottom of yours warm. Still am." A shock of dark hair fell across his forehead, making him look reckless and sexy as sin.

"No, thanks." Looking away from those compelling blue eyes, Lorelei concentrated on pushing her eggs around on the plate. Why did the blasted man have to be so good-looking? And why did the mention of him keeping her warm have to set her pulse to tap-dancing again?

"How are your eggs?" Jack asked, evidently deciding not to continue pushing in the other direction.

"They're fine." Lorelei managed to shovel in another mouthful.

"Good. Because you're going to need your strength. The desert heat isn't the same as the city. It's brutal and will rob every ounce of your energy. And believe me, we're going to need our energy. We've got a pretty full day ahead of us."

Which meant she wouldn't have much time if she was going to get away. "So, you're planning on looking for the mine today?"

"Probably not until tomorrow. We don't have too much farther to go, but we'll need to set up our base camp. Then I thought you might want to look over the map with me and help me decide which section we should check out first."

"You want *me* to help you decide where to search?"

"Sure. You used to like studying the treasure maps with me when we were in Florida and you were pretty good at it. Hell," he said, giving her that sexy grin, "you were better than good. You were terrific."

"How can you say that? We never did go on any of those treasure hunts we talked about."

"I know. But remember that trio of Spanish ships whose course we kept going over to try to figure out where they might have gone down?"

"You mean the ones carrying some noblewoman who'd stolen an heirloom emerald necklace and ring from her dowry and gone to meet her lover?"

"Yeah. That's the one."

"According to the legend, the ships were cut down by the pirates hired by the woman's family to bring her back. Instead, they killed her and sunk the ships."

"And the jewels were never recovered."

Lorelei thought back to those afternoons they had spent studying the journals and their plans to find the missing ships. Unable to stop herself, she grew excited and asked, "Did you really find the ships? And the missing jewels?"

Jack frowned. "No, not exactly." Some of the enthusiasm left his eyes. "I didn't find the mother ship or the jewels, but I did find one of the smaller ones that was carrying a small cache of gold doubloons. It was just off the coast of Florida—right where you swore it would be."

She'd been right. And she'd missed it. A flutter of disappointment settled over her. While it was hard to imagine herself as ever having been so impractical as to consider such a venture, a part of her wished that she had been with him when he'd found the ship. She couldn't help thinking of the sad noblewoman and the man who had been waiting for her. And what had ever happened to the missing jewels? Just as quickly as the question popped into her head, she dismissed her thoughts as foolish. "What does all this have to do with me?"

"Don't you see? I never would have found that ship if it hadn't been for you. And together we can find the Dutchman's Mine. I know we can. It'll be just like it used to be. Just like we planned. You and me. We'll be a team again, and this time it'll be for keeps."

Confused, she fought back the unwanted flicker of emotion his words stirred inside her. "No! We can't go back. *I* don't want to go back. Things are not the way they used to be. We're not the people we used to be. I'm not the same silly girl who fell in love with you ten years ago."

His expression grew hard, determined. "No. You're not. But the woman who kissed me last night is still the same woman who told me she loved me and agreed to marry ten years ago.'' He threw out the remainder of his coffee and stood. ''Go ahead and finish your breakfast. I'll start loading up the truck.''

''Wait!'' Panic shot through Lorelei.

''What?'' He stopped in midstride.

''I'm finished.'' She stood and tossed out the remainder of her own coffee.

''Fine. Then you can clear away the breakfast stuff while I pack the truck.''

Nerves jumping, she said, ''I hate kitchen cleanup, and you know it.''

''Sweetheart, I hate to remind you, but this isn't a kitchen. It's a campsite.''

''I still don't like it. I got stuck doing it often enough growing up.''

''That's because you let your two sisters con you into it.''

It was true, but it was also beside the point. ''I'll pack up our gear and you clean up.''

Jack hesitated. ''All right. I'll go rinse out the dishes in the stream behind those rocks, and you can start loading your stuff into the truck. Don't worry about the tent. I'll take it down as soon as I finish KP duty.''

While Jack gathered up their dishes, Lorelei headed for the tent. Retrieving her backpack, she forced herself to walk and not run to the truck. After dumping her gear into the back seat, she climbed into the driver's seat, not even bothering to adjust the seat to accommodate her shorter legs or to strap on her seat belt.

Her heart raced. The blood seemed to roar in her ears like horses racing around the track in a dead heat. She glanced in the rearview mirror, half expecting Jack to step over the ridge at any moment. She'd send his friends from Tortilla Flats back for him, Lorelei promised herself. Fingers trembling, she fit the key into the ignition and turned it.

The engine kicked over, the sound shattering the mountain quiet, but it didn't catch. Wiping her damp palm on the leg of her shorts, Lorelei turned the key again.

Again the engine simply turned over and died.

Frantic, she turned the key once more and pumped the gas. "Come on. Come on. Start."

Once more it refused to catch.

"It might work better with this."

Lorelei's head whipped to her left, where Jack stood at the truck's open window smiling and holding some thingamabob in his hand.

"Distributor cap," he explained as he pulled open the truck door. He flashed her another infernal grin. "The truck won't start without it."

Fury exploded inside her. "You jerk!"

She lunged out the door for him, throwing the weight of her body at him and knew the satisfaction of hearing his laughter change to a grunt. His arms flailed as he struggled not to lose his balance.

"That'll teach you to play ga—"

Jack snagged her arm, pulled her against him, and then Lorelei's own feet started to slide. "Let me go," she screamed as she felt herself begin to fall.

"Never," he said. Wrapping his arms around her, he captured her mouth with his just before they toppled and went tumbling down the hill.

Jack held Lorelei's body against his as they rolled once, twice, three times before landing at the bottom of the hill. When they stopped, he was lying on his back with Lorelei plastered on top of him, her mouth clinging to his. Jack could feel a small rock at the center of his back that was probably going to leave a nasty bruise.

He couldn't bring himself to care. Not when Lorelei's fingers were curled into his shirt, her breasts pressed so tightly against his chest, her legs tangled between his and brushing his sex. She lifted her head and stared at him out of shocked brown eyes.

"You know, darling, I was only kidding when I made that remark about this being kinky foreplay. Now I'm not so sure it's a bad idea."

"You idiot!" She pushed herself off him, and Jack groaned as he felt the rock dig into his spine. "Of all the stupid things to do. You could have killed us both!" She scrambled to her feet and continued to yell at him.

Apparently even the coyote ranked higher than he did at the moment, Jack mused as he listened to the assorted vermin she compared him to and waited for her to run out of steam. He reached behind him and managed to remove the annoying rock. He dropped down once more, noting that she was beginning to wind down.

"Well, what are you waiting for? Get up," she demanded.

He didn't move, convinced she hadn't quite finished.

She inched closer to him. "Jack, did you hear me? I said to get up."

When he shifted his body to get more comfortable, he groaned. Problem was there wasn't anything comfortable about lying at the bottom of a hill with rocks digging in his back.

"What's wrong? Are you hurt?" Her eyes narrowed, making a tiny line at the center of her brow as anger turned to concern. "Did you break something when we fell?"

"Nothing important." Her lips bunched themselves into a pout. A streak of red dirt slashed across one flushed cheek. Her gold brown hair had escaped the ponytail she'd coaxed it into earlier and now tumbled in a wild mass about her shoulders. Several buttons on her blouse had come undone, revealing a tantalizing hint of cleavage.

"Then why aren't you getting up?" As she stood over him with her feet spread apart and her hands on her hips, her frown deepened. "Or are you just planning to lie there for the rest of the day?"

"Actually that wouldn't be such a bad idea if I could talk you into coming down here to join me. What do you say, sweetheart? Ever made love at the bottom of a mountain before?"

Fire flashed in her eyes, and she aimed her hiking boot for his midsection. Jack caught her ankle before she made contact and tumbled her down on top of him.

"Let me go," she commanded.

"Not a chance."

"You tricked me. You let me steal the truck keys on purpose when you knew the thing wouldn't start." She smacked him on the shoulder with her fist.

"Ouch." Rolling her onto her back, Jack looked down at her mutinous face. "Did you really think I'd trust you? You told me you were going to run away."

She bucked her body against him, which did nothing to ease his rapidly arousing condition. "I've already promised to take you back to Mesa after we find the mine or after the ten days are up—whichever comes first. I have no intention of letting you go before then."

"You have to sleep sometime, Storm, and when you do, I'm out of here!"

She struggled beneath him, and Jack could feel desire stir again. "So do you, sweetheart, and I guess if I'm going to stop you from doing something foolish, I'll just have to make sure that the two of us sleep together."

She angled up her chin. "I'd sooner sleep with a rattlesnake."

As much as he was enjoying the feel of Lorelei in his arms and the verbal sparring, it was long past time for them to be on the road. He kissed the tip of her nose. "You know you don't mean that. You and I want each other, and sooner or later we're going to end up in the same bed."

"Not unless you're planning to force me."

"You and I both know I wouldn't have to force you."

"Force is the only way you'll get me in bed with you."

"Is that a challenge, Lorelei?" He gave her a slow smile. "You know how much I love a challenge."

He caught the quick flicker of uncertainty before she could bank it. "It's a statement of fact. Force is the only thing that would make me go to bed with you."

"It's too bad we don't have the time right now for me to prove what a liar you are. But we really do need to get going. So I guess we'll both just have to wait until later. But if you're interested, I'm willing to make you a little wager that before the week's out, you'll be in my arms, clinging to me and pleading with me to make love to you."

"Be grateful I'm not a gambling woman, Storm, because you'd lose your shirt. Now let go of me."

"I wouldn't mind losing my shirt to you."

She moved her knee to his crotch, and Jack decided the wise thing to do was to get up. After pushing himself to his feet, he held out his hand.

Lorelei smacked it away and came to her feet. She dusted the backs of her legs and shorts and glared at him. "It'll be snowing in July before you'll find me in your arms clinging or begging you for anything."

Eleven hours later it was still July and there wasn't any snow in sight, but Lorelei was definitely in his arms and she was definitely clinging. A pack of coyotes let out another round of howls, and she shuddered and burrowed even closer.

Jack folded his arms more tightly around her and stroked her back. "Shh. Don't worry, sweetheart. They're not going to bother us. I told you, even if they were starving, the fire would keep them away."

"I know. I know. I guess it was coming up on that nest of rattlesnakes earlier."

She shivered again, and Jack pressed a kiss to her temple.

Slowly he could feel her body begin to relax against him. He continued to soothe and to stroke her. "Feeling better?"

"Yes. Thanks," she told him as she lifted her head and looked up at him.

"My pleasure. What do you say we get ready for bed?"

Lorelei nodded. She paused and sniffed at the air. "Do you smell something burning? I mean something besides the wood?"

Jack sniffed, then his body froze. An icy chill raced down his spine. He spun around, and his heart came to a stop as he spotted the map—the key to his and Lorelei's future—lying near the fire, the edges curling in smoke and flames greedily licking at the corners.

Seven

"The map!" Jack pushed her aside and dove to the ground, reaching for the burning map. He began to beat at the flames with his hands.

"Stop it," Lorelei screamed. "You'll burn yourself."

Ignoring her, he continued to bat at the flames with his palms, refusing to stop until the fire was out. When it was over, he simply sat there staring at the map, smoothing his fingers along the charred parchment.

Lorelei's heart swelled and seemed to grow heavier in her chest. Before she could stop herself, she was kneeling beside him, reaching out to touch his shoulder. "Let me see your hands."

"My hands are okay." But he didn't look at his hands. His eyes remained focused on what remained of the map, looking as though he'd just lost his best friend.

"They're not okay," she insisted. "You're hurt."

"It's gone, Lorelei. Part of the map is gone."

The despair in his voice ripped at her. "Will you forget

about the blasted map!'' She snatched the thing from his fingers and tossed it to the ground. When he started to retrieve it, she grabbed his wrists.

''I said to forget about the map. There's nothing you can do about it now,'' she said in the voice she reserved for overexuberant schoolchildren who came into the bookstore. ''Now, let me see your hands.''

Jack lifted his gaze to hers. The anguish she'd heard in his voice was in his eyes. Beating back the urge to open her arms and offer comfort, she looked down at his hands. She turned them palms up. Dirt and traces of ash streaked across the surface. Ugly pink blisters were already starting to form on three of his fingers and the base of his palms. ''Oh, Jack. Look what you've done.''

''It's nothing. Just a little burn. I've done more damage than this working on ships.''

It was probably true, Lorelei decided. His hands were a road map of the physical life he'd led. They were dark, work-roughened and callused hands. Traces of several scars he'd earned during one adventure or another had added to the heart and life lines that crossed his palms. Palms that were now swollen and had a painful shade of red bleeding through the dirt and soot. Angered that he would do this to himself, Lorelei stormed, ''Of all the dumb things to do. You're an idiot for doing this to yourself over a stupid piece of paper.''

He yanked his hands free and picked up the map. ''I'm an idiot, all right—for being careless with this in the first place.''

She didn't bother to argue further. ''Do you have a first-aid kit?''

''I told you it's nothing. I'm all right.''

''And I told you, you're not. That's a nasty burn and in a few minutes it's going to be hurting like the dickens. Now, tell me where the first-aid kit is.''

"In the truck," he said, his gaze fixed once more on the portion of map that remained.

"What about ice? Do we have any left?"

He shrugged. "Probably not."

"Give me the keys."

He hesitated as he looked at her outstretched hand.

Lorelei let out an exasperated breath. "As tempting as the idea is, I'm not about to leave you stranded here and run off with the truck—at least not while you're hurt."

"And I'm supposed to believe you? You've tried to run twice now."

"You don't have any choice. Now, give me the keys." She held out her hand.

"They're in my right pocket." He looked at his hands and then back at her. "You'll have to get them yourself."

When she hesitated, he held his hands up above his head to give her access. Lorelei leaned closer and slipped her left hand into his pocket. She could smell the fire on him, the musty scent of sweat and dangerous male. Her breast brushed against his arm as she attempted to wiggle her fingers into the snug opening. Awareness skipped down her spine. From the sudden flicker in his eyes, she knew that he had felt the jolt, too.

The fact that Jack wasn't holding her or even attempting to touch her did little to ease the sensation that she was playing with a far more dangerous fire than the one that had hurt Jack. She could feel his eyes on her, watching her, wanting her, ready to lick at her fragile emotions and devour her as the flames had licked at the map. Finally her fingers closed around the metal disk. She pulled the keys from his pocket. "I'll be right back."

But before she could move, Jack's arms closed around her and she was cradled against a hard, muscled chest. "I want your promise that you're not going to run."

His mouth was just a whisper from hers. Her heart raced

like a thoroughbred in the last stretch to the finish. Running, she thought, was the wisest thing to do.

His arms tightened around her. "Promise me, Lorelei."

"I promise not to run," she finally managed to say. When he released her, Lorelei raced up the hill toward the truck, not sure if her urgency stemmed from Jack's wince of pain or from her own need to put distance between them.

For the briefest of moments she stood on the hill, stared at the Explorer and the keys in her hand. Promise or no promise, she'd be crazy not to leave while she had the chance. Every hour she spent with Jack it became more and more difficult to resist him. The longer she stayed with him, the greater her chances were that she'd do something foolish. Hadn't she already found her feelings toward him softening?

She looked down to the clearing where Jack sat on the ground holding what remained of the map. A lump rose in her throat. Smart or not, she'd given him her word. Besides, she couldn't leave him—not when he was hurt.

"And you're a first-rate fool, Lorelei Mason," she muttered as she retrieved the first-aid kit. The ice was gone, but the water was still cool. She dunked a cloth in it and then started back down the hill. She'd get another opportunity, she told herself. She simply had to. But right now Jack needed her, and fool that she was, she didn't have the heart to leave him when he needed her help.

Rushing down to the campsite, she put down the first-aid kit and placed the cool, wet towel on top of it. Except for that brief, suspended moment between them, the map had claimed his full attention. Even now, Jack's eyes shifted from the map to another piece of paper. Awkwardly he moved a pencil over the second sheet with his swollen hand.

Lorelei snagged the canteen beside his backpack. "Hold out your hands." When he didn't respond, she plucked the pencil from his fingers and tossed it on top of the map before grabbing his wrist.

His gaze shot up to meet hers, anger striking sparks in his blue eyes as he jerked his wrist free. "I'm trying to jot down what I can remember of the map."

"Well, it's going to have to wait. I need to clean those burns."

"I don't need a nurse, Lorelei."

"Tough," she replied, borrowing his response to her protests. "You've got one anyway. Now, give me your hands."

"I don't give a damn about my hands! Don't you understand? I've got to try to reconstruct what was on the map. Without it we don't stand a chance of finding the Dutchman's Mine."

"Will you forget about the stupid mine. It's not important!"

"It's important to *me*. I told you, that gold mine's my second chance."

There was something bruised and aching in the way he looked at her, and it tugged at her traitorous heart. "You'll find the mine, Jack. Map or no map. If anyone can find it, you can."

Her response seemed to knock the anger out of him. "You really believe that?" he asked, a mixture of hope and fear in his voice.

"Yes." And she did mean it, she realized. If the mine existed, Jack would find it. "After all, didn't you once brag to me that you were the best there was when it came to finding missing treasure?"

"Yeah. That does sound like something I would say."

She poured water from the canteen and began to bathe his hands. "That's because you *did* say it." Thank heavens once she got past the dirt, the burns weren't as bad as they'd first appeared. The left hand was only slightly swollen, and except for a few nasty blisters on his right palm and fingers, he seemed none the worse for the incident. "I also remember hearing you tell some old salt in Florida that was trying to sell you a metal detector that you'd put the Storm instinct up against a metal detector any day."

A smile tugged at his lips. "I guess I was pretty cocky back then."

"You still are."

"Kind of odd that you remembered those things."

She shoved the wet towel into his hand and closed his fist around it. There had been little about Jack Storm that she'd forgotten in the years that had passed, regardless of how hard she had tried. "Probably because that sort of male arrogance made quite an impression on a naive eighteen-year-old. You were so brash and reckless. I suspect it was part of the reason I was attracted to you."

"You were in love with me."

"I was infatuated with you." She removed the towel and smeared ointment onto the burns, then began to wrap his hand with gauze.

Using his free hand, Jack skimmed a finger up and down her arm—and sent tingles of awareness skittering down her spine. "Is that really all it was, Lorelei? Infatuation?"

"Yes," she lied. "You were older, more experienced than me. I found you exciting. I suspect that most young girls would find that combination difficult to resist." Even now, just the touch of his fingers had the nerves jumping in her stomach and the blood pounding in her ears. He was just as attractive, just as lethal to her now as he'd ever been.

"Then you won't mind if I conduct a little experiment to be sure, do you? After all, you're twenty-eight now, not a girl of eighteen."

"What kind of experiment?" she asked warily as she tore off the gauze and taped it into place. She snagged his left hand, which was tracing her earlobe and creating havoc with her nervous system.

"Oh, just a test to see if it's still nothing more than

hormones that made you respond to me the way you did a little while ago or if maybe it was something more."

Her hand trembled as she smoothed ointment on his injured palm. "I don't think any test is necessary. If you'll recall, *you* were the one who kissed me."

"Yeah. But you were kissing me back."

Ignoring him, Lorelei quickly secured the bandage with tape and snapped the first-aid kit shut, anxious to get away. Before she could stand, Jack snared her ankle and tugged her backward and into his lap.

"Jack!"

In a flash he rolled her over and onto her back, trapping her beneath his hard body. His face was no more than a breath from hers, his eyes focused on her mouth. "Jack, let me go," she said, and could have cringed at how breathless she sounded.

"We haven't conducted the experiment yet," he told her as his lips skimmed the corner of her mouth.

"I'm not interested in playing these juvenile games with you," she argued, and ruined it by moaning when his teeth scraped her jaw. She pressed her hands against his chest, felt the rapid beat of his heart and knew that it matched her own. Liquid heat flowed through her.

"Believe me, sweetheart, I'm not feeling the least bit juvenile at the moment."

And neither was she. She was hot and hungry for him. And if she gave into those feelings, she'd be leaving herself wide open for major heartache. She wanted, needed to be safe, she reminded herself. Jack Storm was anything but. Panic shot through her, and she squirmed beneath him, tried to buck him off.

Her action had her hips arching toward him. Jack groaned. Those blue eyes that had seemed so haunted such a short time ago turned to the color of smoke. "No. There's nothing even remotely juvenile about the way you make me feel, Lorelei. I burn up inside just looking at you. I want you to burn that way for me...with me." He lifted her arms over her head and proceeded to make love to her neck. The dark stubble on his face moved against her sensitized skin and set off fires of hunger inside her.

She wanted to protest, but the words died in her throat as his clever mouth traveled west to taste the line of her jaw. Lorelei knew she could pull free from the fist that cuffed her wrists. He wasn't holding her tightly. Not really. All she had to do was tug. But all of her energy seemed centered on whichever part of her body his mouth was sampling. When that hot mouth of his moved to the corner of her mouth again, Lorelei trembled. She grew dizzy with need. With anticipation.

Jack eased his bandaged hand between them and flicked open the top button of her shirt. Her nipples ached, strained against her bra for the feel of his fingers on them. When his hand closed over her, Lorelei whimpered.

"You're wearing too many clothes," he murmured as his fingertip brushed the edge of her breast.

"Don't," she cried out, catching his hand as he reached for the next button on her blouse. She wasn't sure where she found the strength to stop him when every fiber of her being was pleading for him to continue.

She drew in a shaky breath and tried to rein in her own desire. "This isn't what I want."

"Liar. You want me just as much as I want you. And this time it's not because you're a naive teenager."

She couldn't deny it, so she didn't even try. "You're a skilled lover, Jack. It only stands to reason that you can make me want you physically."

"*Want* is a mild word for what we do to each other, Lorelei. Admit it. We still love one another. Another ten minutes, and that fire would seem ice-cold compared to the heat between us."

Lorelei flushed. Even now, she could still feel the burn of his lips and hands on her body. She was all too aware of his hard arousal pressed against her and the treacherous ache inside her that wanted more.

"Make love with me, Lorelei," he whispered seductively. He pressed his lips to the corner of her mouth. "You know that you want to."

"Having sex with you won't change anything, Jack. Wanting you isn't loving you."

"You're in love with me," he insisted.

"I'm in love with Herbert."

She watched the emotions chase across his face—hurt, anger, denial. He caught her chin with his fingertips. Fury glinted in his eyes, turning them almost black. "I could prove what a liar you are," he told her, the softness of his tone somehow making the threat ten times more dangerous than if he had yelled. "And once I was inside you, you wouldn't even be able to remember Herbert's name."

Her blood began to spin. Her knees felt suddenly weak, and she had to fight the urge to give into the need drumming through her veins.

"Shall I prove it, Lorelei?"

She clamped down on the flurry of images his words evoked and forced her voice to remain even as she said, "I know I called you a pirate for shanghaiing me from my wedding. I didn't realize kidnapping also meant rape."

Jack reeled back as though she had struck him. Cursing her, he rolled away and punched one of the sleeping bags. He swore again as he clutched his hand.

Lorelei shot to her feet. Quickly she rebuttoned her blouse. Still shaky from the zing of desire, she took a calming breath before stealing another glance at Jack. He was doubled over, cradling his hand to his chest. "Are you okay?"

When he didn't respond, she knelt down beside him and touched his shoulder. "Let me see your hand." Catching his arm, she turned his hand palm up. Blood seeped through the bandage, staining the snowy white gauze with red. "You're bleeding."

He jerked away from her and gripped his injured right hand. "It's okay."

"It's not okay. You've evidently broken open the blisters. They might even get infected. You'd better let me have a look—"

"I said I'm all right."

She saw his mutinous expression, the hurt her words had caused him. "At least let me change the bandages for you."

"I'll change the bandages myself."

"But I don't mind—"

"But I do. Go to bed, Lorelei," he said as he pushed himself up to his feet. Turning his back to her, he walked off into the night.

He walked and walked along the dark trails with only the aid of moonlight until the ache in his body dulled the ache in his heart. Finally he crawled into the tent exhausted, but sleep continued to elude him. Turning in his sleeping bag, Jack tried once more to rest and blot out thoughts of Lorelei. What a mess he'd made of things. His right hand hurt like the devil. Lorelei had been right. He'd ripped open the blisters when he'd sucker punched his sleeping bag.

But the pain in his hand had in no way compared to Lorelei telling him she loved another man. The real blow, though, had been her use of the word *rape*. He'd never forced himself on a woman in his life. Never had to. And it tore at his gut to have her even suggest that he would do such a thing to her.

Turning over on his side, Jack opened his eyes and looked at her sleeping in the bedroll two feet away. With the aid of the moonlight, he could see the sweep of sooty lashes fan across her pale skin. Her lips were slightly parted, and he could just make out the tiny mole above her lip. Her hair was a tangle of brown streaked with gold that trailed across her cheek and pillow. Desire tightened in his gut as he thought of running his hands through that thick mass and kissing her parted lips.

And she'd probably knee him in the groin if he tried it. Might as well get up, Jack decided, since sleep wasn't an option. Kicking off the covers, he pushed himself to his feet and reached for his jeans. A few moments later he unfastened the flap of the tent and stepped outside into the cool mountain air.

With dawn still more than an hour away, it would be several hours before the temperature reached triple digits again, making now as good a time as any to work on trying to reconstruct what he could remember of the map. Stretching, Jack flexed the fingers of his right hand. They were sore and there was still some swelling, but he'd live. Too bad he couldn't say the same thing about the map. Disgusted with himself, once more he chided his own carelessness. He flexed his fingers again. At least this morning he'd be able to grip the pencil—something he hadn't been able to do successfully last night.

Moving over to the campfire site, Jack tossed a few branches onto last night's remains and struck a match. He waited a moment to watch the flame catch, then went about the task of preparing coffee. As he waited for the brew to heat, he leaned back against a rock and glanced about at his surroundings. The mountains rose up all around him like dark and foreboding beasts ready to pounce. And somewhere hidden within the heart of one of those beasts was his gold mine. Would he be able to find it without the map?

You'll find it, Jack. Map or no map. If anyone can find it, you can.

Lorelei's words came back to him. He had to find the mine. Everything was riding on him finding it. There was no basis for his superstitious belief that without Lorelei he'd never find the mine, and without the mine he would lose Lorelei—other than that inherent feeling in his gut. And his gut told him that without one, he'd never have the other. So he had to find the mine.

And he would have to do it soon because time was running out. He only had six days left to locate the Dutchman's treasure and convince Lorelei that they belonged together. Otherwise, he would lose her forever. The thought left a bitter taste in his mouth.

Reaching for the piece of map he'd taken from his bag, Jack spread it out before him and flipped open the pad on which he'd attempted to jot down what he could remember of the drawing. As he sipped his coffee, he concentrated on trying to resketch what he could from memory.

Deep in thought, Jack didn't hear Lorelei exit the tent. She didn't make a sound or speak a word, but he knew instinctively the moment she moved behind him.

"Did you sleep well?" he asked without looking up from the drawing.

"I... Yes." She paused. "How did you know I was here?"

Jack smiled to himself. Would she believe him if he told her the truth? That his entire body went on alert whenever she was within ten feet of him. Probably not, he decided. It was like radar. The gut feeling that had told him that the map was genuine and had been worth the gamble he'd taken in that card game was the same one that told him that Lorelei was now standing behind him. Instead, he said, "I smelled honeysuckle."

"Honeysuckle?"

"Mm-hmm. Your skin always smelled like honeysuckle to me. It still does. And since there isn't any honeysuckle in the desert, I assumed it was you."

"I, um, I guess it's the body lotion I use."

"Maybe." He continued to pore over the map and refine his sketch. Maybe the lotion had something to do with the way her skin smelled, but he suspected it was a part of Lorelei. Over the years, whenever he had smelled that sweet fragrance, he'd thought of her.

"How's your hand?"

Jack tossed down the pencil and stretched out his fingers. "Better. A little sore, but definitely better." He held it out for Lorelei to inspect.

She ran her fingertips gently along the torn blisters and swollen pads of his hand. "It does look better, but you really should have a bandage over those blisters to protect them and keep out the dirt."

"It's just a couple of blisters, not a knife wound."

"And you don't want to risk getting them infected." She gazed up at him, her eyes warm and concerned. "I'll get the first-aid kit and put a bandage on it for you."

When she came back and proceeded to apply the ointment and bandage to his hand, Jack didn't argue further. He liked the feel of Lorelei touching him. While it was a far cry from the lover's touch that he wanted from her, it was a start.

After she'd finished and packed away the gauze and tape, she said, "Maybe you should postpone your plans to search for the Dutchman's Mine. I mean, with you being injured and losing part of the map."

There was doubt in her voice. "I thought you believed I could still find the mine, with or without the map," he said, trying his best to keep the hurt out of his voice that her words had caused.

"I do. I believe you can do anything you set out to do. I've always believed that." She sighed. "But I'm worried about you. About me. What if you'd been seriously hurt last night?"

"Lorelei, it was only a little burn."

She stood and began to pace. "But it could have been a lot worse. Suppose your shirt had caught fire? Or the tent while we were sleeping?"

Jack stood and came up behind her. He rested his hands on her shoulders, pulled her back to rest against him. "Neither of those things happened. Nothing like that is going to happen."

She turned around to face him, her eyes alive and sparking with emotion. "You don't know that. You can't be sure. These mountains can be deadly." She rubbed her hands up and down her arms. "Do you know what I thought about last night when I saw you battling that fire with your hands? I remembered the stories I've heard about all the people who've died in these mountains looking for the Lost Dutchman's Mine. Thirty-six, Jack. Thirty-six people have died looking for that blasted mine. I don't want number thirty-seven to be one of us."

Jack pulled her to him, stroked her back. He pressed a kiss to her head. "I won't let anything happen to you," he promised. "And I'm too ornery to let something happen to me. It's nice to know that you're concerned, but I have no intention of letting anything happen to either one of us—not when we've got so much time to make up for, so much to look forward to."

She shoved away from him. "I keep telling you, we can't go back. I don't want to go back to what we had. I want to go back to my life in Mesa. Back to Herbert."

Jealousy grabbed him by the throat and squeezed at the mention of the other man's name. He bit back the rage churning inside him. "You ought to be careful tossing Herbert at me, Lorelei. You may have been engaged to him, but you didn't love him—at least not enough to sleep with him."

"And how would you know that?" she demanded, anger making her eyes shimmer like amber.

"Because your sister told me."

Lorelei tightened her lips. "Herbert knew I wanted to wait until we were married. He respected me enough not to pressure me."

"I guess that's the difference between him and me, then. Because I didn't have to pressure you, since neither one of us could wait for the wedding." He moved a step closer, stroked the pulse beating at her neck. "And when we make love again, and we will, we're not going to be able to wait for the wedding that time, either."

Angling up her chin, she glared at him. "I should have left you last night when I had the chance."

"But you didn't, and now it's too late."

"That's what you think," she told him, stepping away from his touch. "The next time I get a chance, you can bet I'll take it."

Her chance came late the next afternoon. After poring over the map and working on resketching the lost section, Jack had gone through the list of clues the Dutchman had left regarding the mine's location. A series of riddles that teased and taunted and made little sense—except to Jack, who was determined to solve the puzzle. "We'll start searching in that section over there to the west," he'd advised her. Reluctantly she had accompanied him into the mountains equipped with food and full canteens to search for the mine.

The heat had been almost unbearable. So had feigning indifference each time Jack had reasoned through another clue and set them off to explore another section of mountain. In truth, she'd been excited by the search and disappointed when they hit yet another dead end. Tired, hungry and hot, she came to a halt. She'd had enough. "I refuse to climb another step," she informed Jack.

He looked down at her from his perch several feet up atop a cliff. "All right. We'll go back to camp right after we check out this last cave."

"No. I'm not climbing another inch of this godforsaken mountain or looking in any more darn caves today. I've had it, Jack. I'm not moving from this spot unless it's to go down."

Taking off his hat, Jack wiped his arm across his brow. As tired and irritated as she was with him, it was impossible not to notice how sexy he looked. Even with a layer of sweat and red-colored dirt streaking across his face and forearms, he was as handsome as ever. Muscles rippled on arms bronzed by the sun. His blue eyes rivaled the darkening sky with their color. With his battered hat, worn jeans and an opened shirt that afforded glimpses of a hair-dusted chest, he was a young girl's fantasy come to life—a sexier, more enticing version of Indiana Jones.

And she'd been out in the sun too long, Lorelei told herself as she felt her pulse pick up speed.

He ran a hand through dark hair dampened by sweat. "Come on, sweetheart, just one more cave," he coaxed, giving her one of those killer smiles of his.

"No. I'm not going another step. I mean it, Jack. I'm beat."

He glanced up at the sun still burning like a million-watt bulb in the sky and then shoved his hat back on his head. "All right. You win," he told her. "We'll call it a day."

But she didn't feel as if she'd won anything, Lorelei thought as they started down the mountain. In fact, she was sorely disappointed since she'd actually hoped they would find the mine.

Not that their fruitless search seemed to bother Jack. He met her brooding silence with a steady monologue about what a great day it had been and how proud he'd been of her for discovering a slot canyon that they'd ended up exploring. "I wish you'd have been with me when I was searching for that emerald in Colombia. I bet I would have found it if you had. You're a natural when it comes to treasure hunting."

But she didn't feel like a natural; she felt...she felt frustrated and let down. Especially since at one point, she had actually thought she'd discovered the mine.

More than two hours later when they reached the base camp, she was hot, hungry and spoiling for a fight. "I suppose you expect me to fix dinner," she told him, tipping up her chin and setting her hands on her hips.

Jack removed his hat and wiped a handkerchief across his brow and face. "It's your turn. I did breakfast."

It was true. He had fixed breakfast for them and even packed their lunches.

"Don't frown, sweetheart. You'll get wrinkles between those beautiful eyes."

Lorelei glared at him, but he only laughed and dropped a kiss on her forehead. "Make it something simple if you want. A sandwich or a can of beans is fine with me. I'll do the cleanup."

"Suppose I refuse?"

Jack shrugged. "Then I'll fix us both something to eat when I get back. I'm going to wash up." Leaving her standing there mad and with no one to fight with, he headed for the creek that ran along the campsite.

After several minutes of studying her food options, Lorelei settled on the canned stew again. Dumping the contents into a pot, she opted for using the camping stove Jack had set up earlier. She flicked a match. Nothing happened. After several more attempts without success, she threw the box of matches down and went in search of Jack.

She found him leaning over the stream, bare to the waist, dunking his head into the water and allowing it to run down his neck and back. Lorelei's breath hitched as she watched beads of water chase one another down those wide, tanned shoulders, forming tiny rivers that sluiced down his back.

"Ah, what the hell," she heard him mutter just before he turned around and unbuckled his jeans.

Lorelei stepped back into the curtain of trees and shrubs. Color rushed to her cheeks as he kicked off his boots and began stripping off his jeans. She shouldn't watch him like this, she told herself. Only a voyeur would do such a thing.

But she couldn't bring herself to move away. Another breath snagged in her chest as he stripped off his briefs. She'd been right, some crazy portion of her mind muttered. His tan *did* extend all over. And with that realization came an unwanted, traitorous flash of desire.

Then Jack was turning around, picking his way through the rocks and wading to the center of the stream. When he was chest deep, he dove into the water.

Lorelei squeezed her eyes shut and caught the image of Jack's golden, naked, wet body entwined with her own. Desire fisted in her belly, seeped between her thighs and made her ache. The sound of water splashing had her opening her eyes and watching as he broke the surface and swam to the other side of the creek.

She dragged in a deep breath. *I have to get away from him,* she told herself, suddenly panicked. She darted a glance to where his jeans lay on a rock. Jack was a good twenty feet from the shore. If she hurried, she might be able to get the keys and make it back to the truck before he could jump into his pants and come after her. She had to do it, Lorelei told herself. She couldn't spend another night alone with him.

Heart thundering, she waited for the right moment, unable to hear, barely able to think over the wild hammering in her chest. When Jack dove below the surface again at the other side of the creek, she dashed over to the clearing and grabbed his jeans from the rock. Fingers trembling, she jammed her hand into one pocket and found the pouch with the wedding rings. She nearly gasped aloud as a slash of sadness went through her.

Shoving the pouch back into his pants, she dug into the other pocket. Her fingertips brushed the metal disk with the keys. She jerked them free and closed them in her fist.

"Lorelei! What in the hell are you doing?"

Her gaze shot up. Jack stood in the middle of the river,

a stunned expression on his face. "I'm sorry, Jack. I'm sorry."

"Lorelei, wait!" She heard the water splash and saw him start to swim toward her.

"I swear I'll send someone back for you," she yelled as she tossed his jeans on the ground and turned to run. She tripped over his boots and fell to the ground, dropping the keys in the process.

She pushed herself up to her knees and winced at the sting of pain. Glancing behind her, she saw Jack reach the edge of the water. A new surge of adrenaline shot through her, and she scrambled to her feet. Snatching up the keys, she started to run.

She made it to the clearing, determined to get back to the campsite and escape with the truck. And then she heard Jack behind her.

"Damn it, Lorelei, come back here!"

He hadn't bothered with his jeans. The absurd thought registered as she tried to outrun him. She'd almost made it to the other side of the clearing when she heard him yell.

Then suddenly she was being tackled around the ankles and dropped to the ground. "Let me go," she screamed, kicking to break free.

"Ouch! Damn it, Lorelei, stop kicking me."

She let out another kick that knocked him on his backside, and he let loose a string of curses.

She'd barely gotten up again when he snagged her from behind and wrapped his arms around her. "Let me go," she demanded as she tried to break free of the arms imprisoning her like a straitjacket.

"No," Jack said as he kept her pressed tightly against him and started moving back toward the rock where his pants were. "What in the hell did you think you were doing?"

"Getting away from you," she informed him as the back of her boot connected with his shin.

"Ouch! Damn it, Lorelei. I said to cut that out."

"No. I'm going back to Mesa."

Still holding her, he reached down to pick up his jeans. "I told you, I'll take you back there myself in another five days."

"I don't want to wait five more days." She didn't think she could spend that much more time with him and not make a fool of herself. Even now, she was far too aware of his nakedness pressed against her. And worse, she was terrified that she was beginning to fall in love with him all over again.

"Tough. You're going to wait anyway. Now, be still," he told her, easing his hold. "Let me get on some pants."

When he attempted to insert one foot into the pants leg, Lorelei jerked free. Jack snagged her arm before she could make another run for it. Reflex had her whirling around and swinging.

He dropped his pants, ducked her fist. "What in the hell's gotten into you?"

He was what had gotten into her. She didn't want to fall in love with him again and she was perilously close to doing just that. Frantic, she continued to swing at him—out of fear, out of frustration with both him and herself.

When her right fist connected with his jaw, Lorelei yelped—but not nearly as loud as Jack. She didn't know who was more surprised—her or him. But she froze the moment she stared at his face, which was dark with determination.

"That does it, you little hellcat." He scooped her up into his arms and started walking toward the creek. "I don't know what's eating at you or why you're determined to maim me, but it's time you cooled off."

Kicking, yelling, she tried to break free as he carried her down the rocks and into the water. "Put me down this instant," she demanded.

"Whatever you say, sweetheart."

Too late she realized his intent. "Jack, no," she cried out just before he dropped her into the water.

Eight

Lorelei came up sputtering. "You bastard," she hissed as she swiped the hair away from eyes flashing with temper.

With the evening sun at her back and the water, a faded shade of green, lapping around her, she was as beautiful as ever. She was also spitting mad and soaked to the skin. "Looks like one dunking wasn't enough to cool you off. Guess you need to take another dip."

She yelled, then lunged at him. Jack barely managed to dive out of the way before her body hit the water a second time. Her head shot to the surface again, and she whipped around to face him. Water streamed down her face and neck. Wet hair the color of ancient gold clung to the sides of her neck and shoulders like a royal cloak. Her generous mouth was pulled into a tight line. Anger had given color to her pale cheeks, and Jack could just make out the trace of freckles across her nose. But there was no mistaking the fire blazing in those brown eyes.

"You're going to pay for that, Jack Storm." She dragged in a lungful of air. "I swear it."

"Yeah? And who's going to make me pay? You?" he taunted, much preferring this spitting-mad Lorelei to the indifferent one who'd accompanied him up the mountain today.

"Yes." She spit out the word.

Crossing his arms over his chest, Jack smiled. "Then by all means, go ahead. Make me pay, sweetheart. Make me pay."

She made another lunge for him. He dodged her human cannonball once more and came up laughing. "I'm still waiting, Lorelei," he teased as her head broke the surface.

But this time when she stood, the water was more shallow. This time it wasn't only her face that snagged his attention, but her body. Her lush, womanly body. His throat was suddenly as dry as the desert as he stared at the ripe breasts molded by her plaid shirt, the hips that sloped enticingly from the narrow waist. Desire licked through him with the speed of a bullet. And he was so busy lusting that he didn't see her move until it was too late.

She slammed into him, sending him sprawling backward into the water. Instinct had him wrap his arms around her and take her under with him.

They both came up coughing and spitting water, and before he could catch his breath, she was coming at him again with both fists. "You jerk. You stupid, arrogant jerk."

Jack caught her hands and yanked her against him. "Be still, Lorelei." Damn it, if his body wasn't responding instantly to the feel of her wriggling against him.

"No," she told him. She wrestled to break free of his hold, which only made matters worse because he was all too aware of the wet-slicked arms pushing against his chest, the curve of her hip jutting into his abdomen, the thrust of her thighs against his maleness.

Biting back a groan, Jack pulled her against him again

and tumbled them both down into the water. He released her and prayed the lack of contact would ease the ache in his groin.

It didn't. Not even the cold mountain water put a dent in his desire. Lord, how he wanted her. When she launched herself at him again, Jack caught the full force of her body blow and took her down with him again.

"Ouch," he yelled as she sank her teeth into his shoulder. Instead of dampening his hunger for her, the move set him even more on edge. "You fight like a girl."

"That's because I *am* a girl. I mean woman," she corrected.

Jack's gaze zeroed in on those breasts rising and falling with her labored breaths. He forced himself to look up into her eyes and attempted a smile. "I can see that."

His words set her off, and she came at him again, but this time when she sank her teeth into his shoulder, he dragged her head up, cupped that beautiful face in his hands and captured her mouth with his. He devoured her—like a starving man—with teeth and tongue and lips.

Her fingers snagged into his hair, curled into fists as her tongue waged war with his. Desire, erupting inside him like the volcanoes that had formed the mountains, made his blood heat like lava. Feeling his control slip, Jack tore his mouth free. Terrified any moment now he would begin begging her to let him make love to her—or even worse, embarrassing himself by not even being able to wait if she were to say yes—Jack lifted her up and tossed her body into the creek. Distance, he decided, was what he needed, and started back toward shore.

Lorelei made an angry, frustrated sound behind him. Water splashed as though she'd slapped it with her fist. He would have laughed if the ache in his lower body weren't so painful. He could have had her. He was almost sure of it. Lorelei had always responded to him and even angry, she'd responded to him just now. But it wasn't just desire and sex he wanted from her, Jack realized. He wanted her love.

Abandoning his swimmer's crawl, Jack stood. Water sluiced down his body and dipped below his waist as he began to make his way toward land. Some pirate he turned out to be, Jack mused. Here was the one woman on the earth that he wanted, and he was walking away from her because he wanted more than the surrender of her body. He wanted her love.

He'd taken no more than a few steps when he heard another splash. He turned around in time to catch Lorelei as she hurled herself at him. "Holy sh—"

She dragged them both down into the water and when they surfaced this time, she started swinging. "How dare you kiss me like that and toss me back in the water like a...a trash fish."

"Lorelei, stop. I—"

She threw a punch. He blocked her blow. She tussled with him, rammed him in the gut and knocked him back into the water. He caught her by the waist and dragged her right along with him down into the shallow water. Her fists tangled in his hair, and he was pretty sure that she was trying her best to rip it from his scalp. But he didn't let her go.

Sun-dappled water lapped at their bodies. Air rushed in and out of his lungs. Trapped in his arms, her body pressed snugly to him, she tried to kick at him. Jack snagged her legs between his own. There was no mistaking his reaction to the movement.

Or hers. Desire sparked in her eyes, turning them the color of burned sugar. Her lips, no more than a breath away from his, trembled.

"Just who is it you're fighting, Lorelei? Me? Or yourself? Because you want me, sweetheart. Just as much as I want you."

She made a frustrated cry deep in her throat and jerked his mouth to hers.

Groaning, Jack rolled her onto her back. He tore his mouth free. "Let me hear you say it, Lorelei. Admit that you still love me."

She responded by biting at his lower lip. She streaked her hands down his back, his hips, his buttocks. He cried out, the sound more an animal growl than that of a human as she switched directions and brushed those clever fingertips over his sex.

"Say it, Lorelei. Tell me you love me."

Then she closed her fingers around him. His vision blurred. He could no longer speak. He could no longer think. And for a moment he was afraid he'd spill into her hand. The words would have to wait, he told himself and set to work on the buttons of her blouse. Icy water washed over their bodies. All Jack could feel was the heat, hot, insistent, burning him from the inside out.

He parted the cotton and unhooked the front of her bra. Her breasts spilled out, perfect and full, into his palms. He licked one dusty pink nipple with his tongue.

"Jack," she gasped, her body arching toward him. Her eyes closed to half slits. Her nails dug into his shoulders.

"Tell me what you want, Lorelei. Tell me," he said as he caught the tip between his teeth.

She shuddered. "Y-your hands. Your mouth," she whispered huskily. "I want them on me."

What little control he had left went up like smoke. Driven by an insatiable need to please her, he suckled, he licked, he closed his teeth over the tip of first one breast and then the other as she clung to him, writhed against him, dug her nails into his back, into his buttocks.

With unsteady fingers he fought with the zipper on her shorts and when he managed to yank the thing down, he felt as though he'd just won a gold medal at the Olympics.

He slid his hand down her stomach, inside the edge of her panties.

She arched her hips. "Jack," she said, murmuring his name in a deep, husky voice that had his body tightening, his blood spinning with need. He wanted her so badly, had dreamed of being with her like this so often, he could hardly breathe.

Forcing himself to move slowly, he eased his fingers through her wet curls and into the mouth of her sex. She cried out and when she sank her teeth into his shoulder, desire—hot and raw— licked through him.

Water splashed nearby, and Lorelei stiffened in his arms. Jack whipped his head to the right. "What the hell!" He shielded Lorelei with his body and glared at the old man several yards away at the water's edge busily filling canteens.

"Don't you folks mind me none," he told them as he fastened the top on one canteen, hooked it to a strap across his shoulder and proceeded to fill the next one.

"What in the devil do you think you're doing?"

Pale-colored eyes that could have been anywhere from fifty to eighty glinted at him beneath heavy brows that brooded over a wrinkled face half-covered by thick gray whiskers. "I think that's pretty obvious, son," he told him. A smile played at the edges of lips parched by sun or age or both. "I'm refilling my canteens before I go back up in them hills. I'll be out of you young folks' way in just a bit, and you two can get back to whatever it is you were doing."

What they'd been doing or about to do was make love. Standing behind Jack, Lorelei had already pulled on her blouse and refastened her shorts. Given her mortified expression and the fact that she refused to even meet his eyes, he was sure she was already regretting what had almost happened between them. "I don't guess there's any chance of that happening, is there?" he asked her.

She flicked her gaze to him for a moment, and he caught a brief ghost of something. Longing? Regret? He couldn't decide. Then she was smoothing her hair away from her face and glancing over at the shore. "Be grateful that old guy came along when he did. Otherwise, we would have made a mistake that we'd both regret." Shoving past him, she headed for shore.

Angry, frustrated, Jack marched out of the water behind her, not the least bit concerned about his nakedness. Hell, he wasn't packing any equipment the old codger hadn't seen before, he reasoned.

Once he was back on land, Jack jerked on his pants and joined Lorelei in the clearing where she had leaned over to pick up the truck keys. "You're wrong—about it being a mistake. We belong together. I keep telling you that."

"And I keep telling you I don't believe in fate. I'm going back to the camp to get into some dry clothes."

When she started to walk past him, he caught her arm. Given the slight tremor in her voice, he knew she was shaken by what had almost happened between them. And he didn't put it past her to try to steal the truck again. "Planning to try to run away again?"

"No. I've decided to stick it out."

The tightness in his chest eased a notch. "Ah, sweetheart. Just wait. You'll see. Once we find that mine, then the two of us can—"

"I'm going along with this…this ridiculous scheme of yours to prove to you that I'm not your good-luck charm and that fate has nothing to do with it. There isn't an 'us,' Jack. And there won't ever be an 'us.' I made the mistake of thinking I was in love with you once a long time ago, but it isn't going to happen again."

Her words cut with the sharpness of a knife. "No? Then what do you call what almost happened back there?" He sliced a glance to where, only minutes before, she'd been clinging to him, her body hot and eager for his touch.

She tipped up her chin and met his gaze squarely. "A lapse in judgment on my part brought on by the heat, hunger and no doubt proximity of an attractive man I once cared about."

"Like hell it was!" Why didn't she just rip his heart out and get it done with? Pride kicked in and stopped him from saying the words aloud. "Sweetheart, you were moaning and begging for me to be inside you."

"I don't moan. And I never beg," she said primly.

"No? In another ten minutes you'd have been babbling and wouldn't have been able to remember your name." He curved his lips into a mocking smile guaranteed to make her back stiffen. "But that's all right, darling. Because I wouldn't have been able to remember mine, either."

Color shot up Lorelei's cheeks. "You're not only arrogant, you're crude."

"Yeah. But I turn you on."

"Think what you like." She tipped her nose up in the air. "Five more days, Jack. Gold or no gold, I expect you to keep your word and take me back to Mesa."

Jack heard the old man's chuckle and sliced an angry glance in his direction. The fellow remained crouched down by the water's edge, slowly filling the string of canteens.

Lorelei jerked her arm free and turned to look at the old-timer still filling his canteens. "He looks like he could use a good meal. Maybe you ought to see if he wants to join us for dinner."

"You're kidding? He's lucky I don't string him up and leave him for the buzzards."

"Jack!"

At her horrified expression, he sighed. "Oh, for heaven's sake. I'm not going to lay a finger on the old geezer."

Her gaze lingered on the old man as he pressed a hand to his back and slowly straightened. "Please, Jack. Ask him to eat with us."

"What's the matter? Don't trust yourself to be alone with

me tonight?'' he taunted. In truth, he was the one afraid. Afraid he wouldn't find the mine. Afraid that without the future it promised, she wouldn't give him a second chance. Afraid that even if he got down on his knees and begged her to stay, she would leave him anyway.

Lorelei let out an exasperated sigh. ''No. I just thought it might be nice to share some intelligent conversation with another human being and discuss something besides lost gold mines for a change.''

She should have known better, Lorelei told herself as she listened to Benjamin Timms spin another tale of his quest for the missing mine. Who but another crazed treasure hunter would be fool enough to spend the month of July in these mountains? From his weathered face and scraggly beard, Ben looked every inch the gold-mining prospector out of the Old West. Right down to the battered, rumpled hat he wore on his head.

''You're a mighty lucky fellow, Jack, that this pretty lady here's willing to put up with your prospecting. Few of 'em are, you know.'' He shoveled down another forkful of stew.

''Lorelei's one of a kind,'' Jack told him. ''I knew she was the only woman for me the first time I laid eyes on her.''

She couldn't help it. Her heart contracted at his words. Could it really be true? Could Jack really love her as much as he claimed?

''If...*when* we find the Dutchman's Mine, I'm going to ask her to marry me.''

Too afraid to look at Jack, afraid if she did, he'd see just how close she was to believing him, she turned toward Ben. ''What about you, Ben? Are you married?'' Lorelei asked.

''Nope. Not now. Had myself a wife once and a little baby gal, too.''

''What happened?'' she asked, and immediately wished

she could take back the question when she saw his fallen expression.

"Afraid my Mary Lou wasn't as strong a woman as you. She was a good woman, mind you. None better. And it was my fault things didn't work out. Not hers." He took a swig of coffee, then stared into the mug as though looking at ghost images only visible to him.

"After the baby came, Mary Lou wanted more security. I guess most women do once the kids come along. Anyways, she'd put aside a nest egg for us to buy this little house she'd set her heart on. A pretty little gingerbread cottage in Alabama." A sad smile twisted his lips. "She was so excited about that place, had all kinds of ideas about decorating and fixing it up."

"What happened?" Jack asked, his voice somber.

"We was set to go to the closing, and I had a chance to buy me a map to the Dutchman's Mine. Not one of those tourist trap things you see everywhere. A genuine map. Even had the paper authenticated." He let out a long breath. "I wanted to use the money to buy the map, but Mary Lou was set against it. We had us a nasty spat about it."

Jack's body had tensed. His eyes had turned dark, brooding, wiping out all traces of the devil-may-care adventurer. "What did you do?"

"I took the money for the house and bought the map. Never did find the mine."

"And your wife?" Jack asked, his voice barely a whisper.

"Left me. Took the baby and went back east. Divorced me a bit later and got herself a job as a schoolteacher."

Jack's shattered expression ripped at Lorelei's heart. "I'm sorry, Ben. How sad for you."

"Like I said—no one to blame but myself. I was just so sure that map would lead me to the mine."

"What about your daughter?" Lorelei asked, trying to

lift some of the sadness that hung in the air like the heat. "She must be all grown up now."

"Wouldn't know. Never saw her again after that. Mary Lou sent me some papers to sign a few years later. Married herself an accountant who wanted to adopt the girl."

Jack's face went grim.

"And you agreed," Lorelei whispered, feeling her heart splinter.

"Seemed the right thing to do."

"I'm sorry, Ben." And she was. She ached for the lonely old man.

He shrugged. "I caused that little girl's mama a lot of pain. Didn't mean to, but I did anyway. Figured I owed her something. Besides, look at me. I've spent fifty of my sixty-four years working at one job or another. Got little to show for it, of course. It's 'cause I never stayed anyplace long and spent most of what I made on treasure maps and getting myself back to this here mountain so I could look for that gold. Now, I ask you, what kind of father would I have made for that kid?"

"I suspect you would have made a very good one," Lorelei told him.

Ben's pale green eyes glistened. He blinked back what she suspected were tears. "I thank you for that, Lorelei. I really do."

"You're welcome."

He tossed out the remains of his coffee and stood. After stretching, he reached for his hat. "I best be on my way now and leave you young folks to yourselves."

"You don't have to go. You're welcome to spend the night here with us," Lorelei told him. She'd made the offer in part because she felt sorry for the old-timer and in part because she wasn't sure she was ready to be alone with Jack. At least not yet. Not when she was feeling the urge to stroke the troubled crease from his brow, to kiss him until he lost that sad look in his eyes.

"She's right, Ben," Jack added. "You're welcome to stay with us for the night."

"Appreciate that, son. And while I've enjoyed you young folks' company and the fine meal, I'm used to being by myself. I find the older I get, the more I enjoy my own company, if you know what I mean."

"But where will you go?" Lorelei asked. "It's already late. You might fall trying to negotiate the road in the dark. You could get hurt."

"Right nice of you to worry, little lady. But you don't have to worry about Benjamin Timms. There's a full moon and a sky full of stars out to guide me. Besides, truth is, I know my way around these hills like the back of my hand. My truck's just up over that ridge there." He pointed to his right. "I got me a little spot where I camp out whenever I come to search in this section of the mountains. Figured it be best if I get settled in. I suspect from those clouds I saw just before the sun went down, that we'll be in for some rain soon. A lot of rain."

"At least it will give us some relief from the heat," Lorelei said. "You're sure you won't stay?"

"Yep, I'm sure. Don't you worry none about me. I'll be fine." He plopped his battered hat on top of his head and hitched the string of canteens over his shoulder. "You got yourself a real prize there, Jack Storm. You be sure to take care of her."

"I intend to," Jack told him. He looked at Lorelei a long moment, his expression even darker, more serious than it had been earlier. Then he reached for the strap of Ben's canteens. "Why don't I carry these up to your truck for you? I need to stretch my legs a bit. I want to get in a little practice for our climb tomorrow."

"Well, now." He scrubbed at his beard. "Seeing's how you put it that way, I don't see how I can rightly refuse helping a fellow prospector now, can I?"

Jack took the heavy burden from the old fellow's shoulder and put it on his own.

"Goodbye, Lorelei." Ben tipped the brim of his hat to her.

"Goodbye, Ben. And good luck."

"I'll be back in a few minutes," Jack told Lorelei. Turning, he started up the rock path after Ben.

By the time Jack returned, she'd cleaned away the remains from their dinner and had rolled out both of their bags in the tent.

"I thought you'd be asleep by now," Jack told her.

"I was just getting ready to turn in." She'd changed into the soft denim shirt she'd confiscated from Jack to use for sleeping and slipped into the folds of the bag. It was the first time she'd been alone with him since they'd nearly made love in the creek. She'd half expected him to attempt to seduce her again and admitted to herself that it probably would have taken little effort. A part of her wanted him to come to her, to touch her, to kiss her, to make love to her. Another part of her was terrified that he would.

He fidgeted with his backpack, brooded over the map. Lorelei tossed and turned, waiting, wanting. Unable to sleep, she sat up and glanced over at Jack. He was still completely dressed, sitting on his bedroll, holding the treasure map in his hand. As though sensing her gaze, he looked up. Lorelei's pulse picked up speed at the hunger, at the heat in those blue eyes.

He jerked his gaze away. Shoving a hand through his hair, he stood and started out of the tent.

"Where are you going?"

"Outside for some air."

"Aren't you going to come to bed?" she asked, and wondered how that needy voice could possibly be hers.

Keeping his back to her, he said, "I want to go over the map again before we set out in the morning."

"It's late, Jack. Why not wait until morning and come to bed?"

He whirled around to face her. Her skin burned at the flash of desire he leveled her way. "Is that an invitation to share *your* bed, Lorelei?" he asked, his voice dangerously soft.

Lorelei swallowed. She clutched at her throat. What was the point in denying it any longer? She'd have to tell Herbert, of course. She couldn't marry him now. Not when she still hungered for Jack. He'd been her first lover. Her only lover. She'd loved him and wanted him ten years ago. She wanted him now. But this time she was older, wiser. She wouldn't delude herself into believing what they shared was love. She wouldn't allow herself to love him. "I...I want you," she said, spitting out the words before she lost the nerve to do so. "What would be the point in denying it after what happened this afternoon?"

Jack came to her, dropped to his knees beside her. He skimmed a fingertip across the pulse beating too fast in her neck. He eased the finger down her collarbone, to the front of the shirt, and stopped at the top button. "Tell me, exactly what is it you're offering, Lorelei?"

"An affair." There. She'd said it—barely—because she could hardly breathe with him so close to her, with those clever fingers toying with her shirt buttons. Her blood started to spin as he slowly eased open one button.

"An affair," he repeated, and Lorelei bit down on her lip to stop from crying out when he eased open a second button and then a third, gently brushing her breasts as he did so.

"Yes," she whispered, and closed her eyes as he drew a line down the center of her breasts. Her breath hitched, and her throat burned as his finger slowly stroked the underside of her breasts.

"Sorry. Afraid I won't be able to accommodate you," he said, pulling her shirt together.

"What?" Lorelei's eyes shot open.

"I said I'm not interested in just sex."

Color rushed up her cheeks. He made it sound so cold, so empty. She hiked up her chin. How dare he make her feel cheap this way? "And what's wrong with just sex? It's what we shared ten years ago. It's what you wanted just a few hours ago."

His lips tightened and temper darkened his eyes. "Ten years ago I was too young and stupid to realize just what I had. It wasn't just sex for me back then and it wouldn't be just sex between us now—not on my part."

"What is it you want from me?" she asked, frustrated.

"What you gave me ten years ago. Your love."

She hugged her arms to herself and dropped her gaze. "I'm not sure I could give you that even if I wanted to."

"Then we've got a problem, sweetheart. Because I'm afraid I'm not willing to settle for anything less." Standing, he moved to the tent opening.

She couldn't believe it. He'd turned her down. Furious, she picked up the hiking boot beside her bedroll. It whizzed past Jack's head and struck the flap of the tent.

"Good shot, sweetheart. But I'm afraid your aim's off."

"Go to hell, Jack."

Nine

He felt as though he'd been to hell and back, Jack decided as he came to another dead end. He threw down his backpack and sat down at the entrance to another slot canyon, heedless of the rust-colored dust and the jagged edges of rock at his back. He dropped his head into his hands and squeezed his eyes shut.

The image of Benjamin Timms filled his mind's eye again. Thoughts of the old prospector had plagued him as he'd headed back to the camp the previous night, and they'd still been with him throughout most of the day. The old man's story had hit him like a freight train. Hadn't he been following a similar path? He'd lost Lorelei ten years ago because he'd opted for a chance at making the "big find" instead of meeting her as they'd planned. How many times had he cleaned out his savings to buy one more chance at the mother lode? Hadn't he even put off buying that boat business he wanted just to chase after the Dutchman's Mine? To try one more time to strike it rich?

Thirty years from now would he be like Ben Timms—alone, lonely, a man whose life had been wasted searching for elusive treasures and neglecting the real treasures until they were lost? Icy fear clawed its way up his spine because he could all too easily see himself in the other man.

How had he let ten years slip by arrogantly believing that simply because he still loved Lorelei, she would feel the same way about him? Oh, he could seduce her. He'd set out to do just that, and for all that he'd succeeded. Finding her waiting for him last night in the tent—so soft and beautiful, nerves jumping as she'd reluctantly admitted that she wanted him—should have thrilled him. It was what he'd wanted. He'd been half-crazy with desire for her and would have gladly turned over the Dutchman's map just to be able to slide himself inside her sweet warmth again.

But she'd offered him an affair—not love. And he'd felt every bit the arrogant bastard she'd accused him of being. He'd realized then that seducing her, having her surrender her body to him, would never be enough. He wanted what he'd lost. He wanted her love.

So he'd angered her deliberately, afraid if she looked up at him out of those hungry, whiskey-colored eyes again, he wouldn't be able to walk away. And she'd paid him back for it in spades today, he thought, grimacing. She'd done so with each cool, remote look she'd tossed his way, with each clipped response.

Maybe it was better this way, he reasoned. At least with her glaring at him and barely speaking, the temptation to touch her, to kiss that frown from her lips, to make promises to her he didn't know if he could keep, had been kept under control. How could he even think about asking her to marry him with nothing to offer her?

He couldn't. But if he could find the mine, then he would have something to offer her—a start for the two of them. He wouldn't have to come to her empty-handed as he had the first time. He'd beg her to forgive him and ask for her love. Surely there was still love in there for him somewhere. He knew Lorelei. She would never give herself easily. If she desired him, she must still care for him. And if he could win her love again, he'd offer her what Ben Timms had foolishly failed to offer his wife. He'd give up treasure hunting for good. He'd buy the boat business and become a respectable businessman, someone she could be proud of.

But first he had to find the mine. Removing his hat, he wiped the sweat from his brow and walked over to where Lorelei sat perched on a boulder looking up at the sky. The glaring sun had been chased behind a curtain of clouds, easing the suffocating heat.

"Any luck?" she asked, favoring him with another wintry look.

"No," Jack admitted. He sieved a hand through his hair. "I was so sure we'd find the mine here. All the clues, the map, everything points to this area. I can feel it in my gut."

"And your gut's never wrong," Lorelei said coolly.

"Not about the things that matter. Not about my feelings for you. I do love you, Lorelei."

"Don't." Some of the stiffness went out of her. She turned away from him to stare out at the canyon. "Don't do this to me, Jack." There was exhaustion in her voice.

"I can't help it," he whispered, coming to stand behind her. He squeezed her strong shoulders. "I'm in love with you. Hopelessly, desperately so."

A breath shuddered through her, and he eased her back to lean against him. "How in the world am I supposed to respond to that?"

"I'm hoping that if...that when we find the mine, and I ask you to marry me, you'll respond by telling me you will because you love me, too."

"You didn't want me last night."

"I wanted you, Lorelei. Last night. Last month. Last year. I want you now. I want you always." He turned her to face him, pushed a strand of hair behind one ear. "I want you more than a starving man wants food."

"Then why did you turn me down?" He heard the hurt in her voice, saw it in her eyes before she dropped her gaze.

He caught her chin, lifted it so he could see her face, so she could see his. "Because you offered me your body, and it wasn't enough. I want...I need you to love me, Lorelei."

"I loved you once, and look where it got me. You jilted me. You broke my heart, and I lost..." She drew in a deep breath and pulled away from him. Turning, she stared out over the mountains. "I don't want to ever open myself up for that kind of hurt again."

Temper, brought on by guilt, spiked inside him. "Damn it, Lorelei, look at me. I did *not* jilt you. I made a mistake. A mistake I sincerely regret. But I told you what happened. If you hadn't been so stubborn and refused to speak to me when I called, I would have explained it to you then and we wouldn't be standing here now arguing about something that happened ten years ago."

"Do you know why I didn't talk to you, Jack?" she asked, her voice deadly calm, her eyes impossibly cool.

"Because I hurt you. Something for which I've already apologized." Frustrated, he drove a hand threw his hair. "Jesus, don't you think I would take it back if I could?"

"But you can't take it back. That's the problem. Yes, I was hurt, Jack. Terribly hurt. But I was also scared to death."

That stopped him cold. "Scared? Why would you be scared?"

She didn't answer.

"Lorelei, why were you scared?"

"I was pregnant." She spit out the word. "I was carrying your child."

His knees felt weak, and for a moment he thought they would buckle. "How?" he asked, and immediately chided himself for the foolish question. "Scratch that. I know how. But why didn't you tell me?"

Tears filled her eyes. "Because I didn't want you to *have* to marry me."

"Have to—" He bit off an oath. "Lorelei, I *wanted* to marry you." He swallowed over the lump lodged in his throat. He was a father? He had a child? "The baby? Did you—?" He couldn't bring himself to ask the question.

"No," she snapped. "I...I lost it. I miscarried the next week after...after you didn't show up for the wedding."

Jack's stomach pitched. He scrubbed a hand over his face. He started to reach for her, but let his hand fall. "God, you must hate me. *I* hate me."

"Don't. I don't hate you, Jack. I—"

A gust of wind whipped through the canyon and set the rust-colored dust to swirling around. Jack drew her to him, shielding her eyes and face from the stinging dust. Squinting his eyes, he looked up at the sky. Heavy clouds glowered overhead like dark, angry puffs of smoke.

"What is it?" she asked, drawing back to survey their surroundings. "What's wrong?"

"Rain."

"So? We could use a break from the heat."

"Not this kind of rain. We need to get out of here." Damn, they should have already started back to the camp. Now it was probably too late. They'd never make it in time. Thunder rumbled in the distance like a loud disgruntled beast, confirming his worst fears. Rain was definitely on the way—but not just a quick shower. "We're not going to be able to make it back to camp before the rain hits. We need to find a place to hole up."

He didn't want to scare her, but he was liking the looks of that sky less and less. A flash flood. The air was ripe with the scent of the brewing storm, and he felt that quiver in his belly again. He had to get them to safety. "I need you to follow me back up along that ridge over there,'' he instructed. He hoped he could find a cave on the other side.

Lorelei glanced at the narrow ridge that slanted to a crease and ran down the rugged mountainside to a ravine below. She looked back at him. ''The path's too narrow. We'll never make it without falling.''

''I won't let you fall,'' he told her. ''Hold on to my hand.'' They had to hurry. The first drops of rain were beginning to fall and splatter against the dry rocks and earth. Within minutes the wind would be whooshing through the canyons, hurling the rain at them like pellets.

Jack pressed his body against the rough rock and moved his feet slowly along the path. His fingers felt numb from Lorelei's tight grip on his hand. ''You okay?'' he asked as the rain and wind picked up even more speed.

''I...I'm scared.''

''You're doing fine. Just a little farther,'' he told her. He could just make out that jutting in the rock. Another slot canyon. He suspected and prayed he was right about there being a cave on the other side.

Just as they made the turn on the ridge, the heavens burst open, firing icy blasts of rain at them like bullets from a machine gun. Water gushed down the mountain, breaking away loose rocks and tossing them into the ravine below. Jack's heart thundered in his chest as they inched along.

He could feel Lorelei drooping under the weight of her backpack and the pounding rain. ''Give me your pack,'' he yelled out to make himself heard above the howl of wind and rain.

''I can handle it.''

But he didn't think she could—at least not for much longer. The wind and rain lashed at them, whipped the hat from his head and sent it sailing down the jagged rocks and into the rugged canyon below. Water rushed fast and hard down the steep mountain slope before plunging wildly into the ravine. It was moving too fast. They would never be able to make it to higher ground. He had to find someplace else.

Carefully they moved along the ridge's edge and stopped under an overhang. With a slight reprieve from the relentless hammering of rain, he searched the mountain wall just to their right. He caught sight of what looked like another cleft in the rock face. Jack swiped the water from his eyes. Adrenaline pumped in his veins, and he felt the prickling along the base of his neck again.

A cave. There was a cave tucked in the shadows of the fissure that cut through the slab of rock. They could hold up there—if they could reach it.

The path that they were on ended several feet short. They had no choice. They'd have to jump and pray the ridge on the other side would hold under their weight. He looked at Lorelei again. Despite the fight still burning in her eyes, she was fading fast. "Do you think you can manage to get to that spot over there?" He motioned to the other hillside.

"How?" she asked, blinking back the rain that streamed in rivulets down her face and body. "This ridge doesn't go that far."

"We'll need to get as close as we can and then jump across to the other side."

She looked at the crumbling rock and back at him. "I'm willing to try anything if it means getting out of this rain."

"That's my girl," he said, pressing a kiss to her wet lips. "I'll go first and once I'm on the other side, you can jump and I'll be there to catch you."

Lorelei nodded. When he started to move, she caught his arm. "Be careful, Jack. I'd hate to see you fall down the mountain and smash up that pretty face of yours."

"Don't worry. I've got my good-luck charm with me, remember? Nothing's going to happen to me." Praying he was right, Jack moved the last few feet to the edge of the ridge. He looked at the crevice on the other side and was more sure than ever that there was a cave.

Lorelei touched his shoulder. "Jack, it's awfully wide. Do you really think you can make it?"

He caught her hand, kissed her fingers and gave her a smile. "Piece of cake," he assured her with a confidence he didn't feel. "I've jumped creeks wider than this little stretch."

"Liar."

"Scout's honor." He held up his fingers.

She chuckled. It was the first smile he'd seen on her face all day. "You were never a Boy Scout."

"That's beside the point. I *have* jumped creeks wider than this." But he'd been twenty years younger and had done so with the sun shining high in the sky. And he hadn't had an avalanche of rain at his back and the jagged teeth of a mountain waiting below to swallow him in its jaws.

He'd never make it with the backpack, Jack decided. Removing it from his back, he thought of the map inside and all of the dreams and hopes that he had tied up with it. And it had been his crazy dreams of buried treasure that had cost him the life of his child.

"Are you okay?"

He shook off the sick feeling in his stomach. "Yeah. Just lightening my load."

"What about the map? Shouldn't you take it out first in case...in case the pack falls?"

"No point. I lost the plastic casing in the fire, and I'm soaked to the skin. I'd only ruin it if I tried," he called out above the wail of the wind. "I'll just have to hope the pack makes it."

"What if it doesn't?"

"Then I'll worry about it later." Gripping the pack, he pitched it across the gap toward the other ridge. It landed on the ridge, teetered a moment, then plunged down the mountainside. Jack's stomach fisted as he watched it disappear into the swirling jaws of russet-and-gray rocks below.

With it went the map and what remained of his dreams to find the mine and build a new life with Lorelei. He'd lost those anyway, he admitted. Even if by some miracle she would forgive him, he didn't think he could forgive himself. It was a moot point any way he looked at it. If they made it through this, he could never ask her to marry him now. Aside from the fact that she had every reason to hate him, he had nothing to offer her. Even if he was able to get a loan to buy the boat business, it would take years before he'd see any serious profit. No. He couldn't come to her with nothing more than his dreams and promises a second time.

"Jack!"

He whipped around at the urgency in her voice, shaking off the self-pity. There'd be time enough to deal with that later—once he had Lorelei safe.

"We need to hurry," she said, her eyes bright with fear. "The ridge behind us...i-it's started to break away."

He sliced his gaze to the path they'd been on not ten minutes before. Water gushed along the surface, breaking off chunks of russet-and-gray rock as it sped down the mountainside.

Terror gripped his heart with a pair of steel fists. They had two, three minutes at best before the water reached them. He had to get Lorelei out of harm's way. He caught her face in his hands and kissed her hard and fast. "Whatever happens, please believe that I love you. I always have." Turning, he leapt across the yawning gap.

The toe of his boot caught the edge of the ridge and then it began to crumble. Lorelei screamed as his foot slipped and his body slammed against the rock, smacking the side of his head in the process.

"Jack! Jack!"

Dazed, he shook his head to clear the stars dancing in front of his eyes. "I'm okay," he yelled back. Holding on to the jutting stone he'd grabbed, he began dragging himself up to the cliff inch by inch. Pain knifed through him as he pulled himself up the jagged surface. A platoon of jackhammers was trying to drill holes in his head. Blood mixed with rain ran down his arm; he felt something warm and sticky seeping at his left temple.

I have to make it to the cliff. I have to do it so I can save Lorelei. He repeated the chant to himself, over and over, as he forced himself to ignore the pain and pull himself up and over the boulder. Willing strength into his arms, he lifted himself up, over the rock and onto the cliff.

He ached and he was still dizzy, but there was no time to lose. "Throw me your pack, Lorelei."

She did so. He caught it and tossed it behind him at the mouth of the cleft. "All right. I want you to move fast but as carefully as you can to the edge of the ridge."

She started to move, and Jack watched the water bulldozing down the path behind her. "You're doing fine. All right," he said as she stood at the rim. "I'm going to count to three, and on three I want you to jump and stretch your arms out toward me as far as you can." Jack took a deep breath, did his best to ignore the pain in his head and shoulder. "Okay. Ready?"

"Ready."

"One. Two. Three!"

Jack's heart froze as Lorelei leapt toward him. Her feet hit the ridge and skidded off the wet surface. "Jack!"

He grabbed her wrists. Her body dangled over the narrow gap that plunged to the deadly rocks below.

"It's no use. You can't hold me. If you do, w-we'll both fall."

She was crying, but through the haze of blood and rain, he couldn't make out where the rain ended and the tears streaking her face began. "I'm not letting you go."

His arms ached under the strain. His ribs and chest hurt where he'd wedged himself behind the rock for leverage.

He dug in his boots and began to lift her. "Look at me, Lorelei. Look at me!"

With her eyes pinned on him, slowly he began to bring her up. He'd never spent a lot of time in his life praying, had long ago decided he probably wasn't a candidate for heaven. But he prayed now, calling on a ghost of a prayer—the only one he could remember—that his mother had taught him as a boy so many, many years ago.

Guardian angel, hear my prayer.... He repeated the prayer over and over in his head and asked for the strength to save the only treasure that had ever really mattered to him—Lorelei.

When her shoulders reached the base of the stone, she scrambled for a foothold and helped bring herself up the rest of the way. Jack wrapped her in his arms and pulled her to the other side of the rock. Her body trembled against him, and he winced as she clutched him.

She drew back and looked up at his face. "Are you all right?"

"Never better," he lied, and tried for a grin. Putting his arm around her shoulder, he said, "Come on. Let's see if I was right about that cave. I don't know about you, but I think I've had my fill of rain for today."

She slipped her arm around his waist, and he urged her into the crevice that split through the mountain cliff. They followed a narrow, curving path, and sure enough, not more than twenty feet from the ridge where they'd both nearly lost their lives was the cave.

"Looks like you were right," Lorelei told him as they reached the mouth of the cave.

"It's the Storm instinct. It never fails," he bragged. He gave her a wink and a smile, then collapsed at her feet.

Lorelei bathed the knot on the side of Jack's head with the T-shirt she'd been wearing under her shirt. She stared at his bruised face, pale beneath the tan, and brushed her fingers over the dark hair curling across his forehead. When he'd fallen at her feet, she'd been terrified he was dead. In those few moments she'd wished she was, too—because she'd realized that for all her fears and protests, for all the anger she carried inside her over their failed romance, she still loved him. Finally she'd been able to admit the truth to herself. She'd always loved Jack and always would.

What a disgusting and nasty thing hindsight could be, she thought. It had taken nearly losing him for her to be able to face the truth. And now that she had, she'd been unable to tell him. How she'd managed to drag him inside the cave, she still wasn't sure. All she'd known was that she couldn't let him die—not now when their whole life was still before them. Not before she could tell him how much he meant to her.

That's what hurt the most, that she'd held back the words from him on the cliff when he'd told her he loved her. He'd asked her for another chance, but she was the one who wanted a chance—a chance to tell him, to prove to him that she loved him.

She swiped at the tears clouding her vision and leaned over to check the bandages she'd applied to the gash on his arm and his side. At least her hands weren't shaking anymore, she noted and congratulated herself. Too bad she couldn't say the same thing about her insides.

Please, please, God. Let him wake up. She didn't know what time it was. She'd lost her watch somewhere on the ridge, but judging from the dark sky amid the steady rain, she was sure the moon was up there somewhere.

And Jack had been out cold for several hours now. Long enough for her to retrieve her backpack and get the small first-aid kit Jack had packed in each of their bags. Long enough for her to strip off his clothes and treat the cuts and scrapes on his body and bandage the more serious wounds. He'd slept through it all—including her tugging off the remainder of his clothes and her own to wrap them both in the thin blankets that had remained dry thanks to the waterproof lining of her pack.

Even the small fire she'd built for warmth hadn't made him stir. How long had he been out now? An hour? Two? Three? Too long, a voice inside her head whispered. Lorelei could feel the panic knotting her stomach again. "Please, Jack. Please, darling, you need to wake up."

Blinking back tears, she gathered a few more of the sticks she'd found at the mouth of the cave and fed them into the fire. Jack groaned. Dropping the sticks, she raced back to his side. "Jack? Jack, can you hear me?"

He moaned again, and his eyes fluttered open. "Lorelei." Her name was barely a whisper on his lips.

"I'm here, Jack. I'm here." She clutched his hand in hers.

He tried to move to sit up. Wincing, he abandoned the effort and rubbed at his head. "God, I feel like I've been hit by a truck."

"No. A mountain," she informed him as she gently stroked his face. "There's some aspirin in the first-aid kit. Do you think you can swallow them?"

"Yeah. Just help me to sit up."

After doing so, she retrieved the pills and her canteen and hurried back to him. She handed him the aspirin and lifted the canteen to his lips. He drank his fill and lay back again.

"What happened?" he asked.

After putting the canteen aside, she tucked the blanket around him. "What's the last thing you remember?"

"The truth?"

"Yes."

His mouth attempted what she thought was a smile, but turned into a grimace. "Praying to my guardian angel to keep you safe."

Lorelei arched a brow. "Someday you're going to have to explain that to me."

He caught her fingers as they stroked his forehead and brought them to his lips. There was an emotional intensity burning in his eyes as he met her gaze. "I owe one to my guardian angel. He came through for me. Because unless I've died and gone to heaven—a place I'm not too sure I'd be welcome—you're here. You're safe. And no one has ever looked more beautiful than you do right now."

"Oh, Jack." She couldn't help it. Her heart stuttered. She didn't need a mirror to know just how disheveled she looked. She was wrapped in an olive green blanket, her body was bruised, her hair was a wild riot of curls around her head and she didn't have a lick of makeup to camouflage her face's imperfections. And he thought she was beautiful. "I'm afraid that crack to your head must have affected your eyesight."

"My eyesight's fine. You'll always be beautiful to me. Always."

"Thank you." The phrase was inadequate at best, but she knew he'd meant every word. She'd never considered herself beautiful. Her sisters had been the real beauties of the family. At the most, with the art of cosmetics she could make herself pleasant looking, even attractive at times. But Jack had always made her *feel* she was beautiful.

"I'm sorry, Lorelei," he said, squeezing her fingertips.

"For what?"

"For everything. For letting you down ten years ago. For not being there with you when you lost our baby. For nearly getting you killed."

She cupped his face in her hands. "Thanks to you, I'm alive. I love you, Jack. Whatever else happens, I want you to know that." When he started to speak, she pressed her lips against his. "Do you know what my two greatest fears were when I was dangling on that mountain and thought I was going to fall?"

"What?"

"That I'd never get a chance to tell you that I *do* love you."

He closed his eyes a moment. "I don't deserve your love. Not after what I did to you."

"You didn't *do* anything to me. You're always the one talking about fate, Jack. The baby..." She swallowed because thoughts of the child they'd lost would always be accompanied by pain. "Maybe the baby wasn't meant to be. But I think you're right. Fate has given us a second chance. I love you, Jack. I love you."

Lorelei smiled as he let out a long breath and opened his eyes. "Aren't you going to ask me what my second fear was?"

"What was your second fear?"

"That I'd die without ever having you make love to me again."

The taste of danger was still in her mouth. Their problems of surviving weren't over yet—not by any means. They were trapped in a cave, a flash flood had wiped out a portion of the mountain trail and they had enough rations to last them two days at best. If she were going to die, she wanted it to be in his arms. She wanted to know at least one more time that thrilling free fall of being loved by Jack. "I want you to make love to me, Jack."

Ten

"But right now you need to rest. We both do. We should try to get some sleep." She tucked the blanket around her and settled down beside him.

Jack leaned up on one elbow. "You expect me to sleep after *that?*" The woman he loved, had always loved, had just told him she loved him and wanted to make love with him. And he was supposed to simply turn over and go to sleep?

She gazed at him, her brown eyes shimmering like a finely aged bourbon. She patted his cheek. "Yes. By tomorrow you'll feel stronger and can do something about it."

Jack rolled over on top of her, caging her body beneath his. "Sweetheart," he said, practically growling the endearment, "believe me, I'm feeling plenty strong enough to do something about it right now."

She stroked his face, pressed her fingertips to his bruised chest. His blood turned to lava under her gentle caress.

"You were almost killed. You've got more cuts and bruises on your body than I could even begin to count. You've still got a nasty bump on your head and you were unconscious for hours," she whispered, the worry in her voice evident. "I was so afraid you weren't going to wake up."

Her concern touched him, humbled him. "I know. I know. But I'm awake now. And while I may have a few bumps and scrapes, as far as I can tell, all my essential equipment is still in working order." To prove his point, he pressed his lower body, already hard and eager, against hers. He smiled at the surprise in her eyes.

"Evidently it is," she murmured huskily. "But I still don't think you should—"

"I want you, Lorelei. More than I've ever wanted anything in my life. I know we're in a hell of a fix here. We need to find a way to get off this mountain, and there are a lot of things you and I will have to work out when we do, but right now I don't want to think about any of those things. I *can't* think about any of those things," he admitted. "All I can think about is the two of us—you and me. Right now. And how much I love you."

"Show me, Jack. Show me." Parting the folds of her blanket, she offered herself to him.

Blood pumped in his veins as he peeled away the rest of the blanket and unveiled all that soft, creamy skin. How many nights had he lain awake on the floor of some jungle, on the hard bunk of some ship, in the bed of his empty apartment in Florida, and dreamed of seeing Lorelei again like this? How many nights had he lain a stone's throw away from her sleeping in the tent and envisioned her like this? The reality was ten times more wonderful than any dream.

Firelight flickered on the walls of the cave, painting her body in a golden hue far richer than any treasure he could ever hope to find.

And she was his.

"Touch me," she whispered.

Desire torched, fired through him, making his hands shake as he skimmed a finger along her throat and forced himself to move slowly. She was like satin, he thought—soft, smooth, exquisite.

"You're so beautiful," he murmured as he continued to explore her, tracing the curve of her breasts, the dip at her waist, the flare of her hips. Lowering his head, he repeated the journey with his mouth. "You taste like honeysuckle," he told her as he licked her neck, then moved to her breasts.

She trembled as he continued to taste her with his tongue. Gently he closed his teeth over the tip of her breast and drew the nipple into the wet heat of his mouth.

"Jack!"

He heard her breath hitch, watched her eyes roll back in her head as she arched her body toward him, curled her fingers into his shoulders.

"Jack, please. Please, I want you inside me."

"Not yet." He wanted to make it special for her. Show her how much he cherished her, how much he adored her. Sweat broke out across his brow as he struggled to keep rein on the need to sink himself inside her, to feel those soft, silken thighs wrapped around him.

He held himself back as he journeyed down her rib cage, tasting every inch of her. She writhed beneath him as he pressed his mouth to the inside of her calf and moved up to her thigh. He parted her with his fingers, and she ran onto his hand hot and wet and sweet like honey. He lowered his head to taste her, caressing her with his tongue and his mouth until she was trembling beneath him and crying out his name.

The storm raged an angry war outside of the cave, rattling the earth with its power and fury. It didn't even come close to matching the desire raging inside him. Unable to wait a second longer, he moved between her thighs and buried himself inside her.

Lorelei arched her hips, taking him deep, deep, deeper inside her. His vision hazed at the sheer pleasure. Then he began to move inside her with long, fast, delicious strokes that seemed to race along with the storm into the night. His heart beat with dizzying speed as he felt them racing together toward some dangerous cliff.

"Open your eyes, Lorelei. Let me see your eyes," he commanded as they sped closer to that jagged edge. "I need to know that this time it's not a dream. That this time you're real. That you're really mine."

"Yours," she whispered, meeting his urgent thrusts. When she wrapped her legs around him, Jack felt them both begin to spin at breakneck speed. "Only yours," she called out as her body convulsed around him.

"Mine," he repeated, and holding her to him, he soared with her over the edge.

Lorelei stretched. She smiled at the delicious aches and tender spots on her body, recalling with vivid clarity how she'd gotten each and every one of them. Had loving Jack been this wonderful the first time around? She wondered, and decided it had not. She looked over at him sleeping beside her, and her heart swelled. Lord, how she loved him. They'd wasted so many years, lost so much time.

At some point they would need to talk. Really talk about the baby they'd made together and lost. He'd mourn the loss of their child as she had. She rubbed at her heart, feeling the familiar ache in her chest as she thought of that dark time. She'd been wrong not to tell Jack and allow him to share that grief with her. But surely there would be more babies in their future.

Not wanting to disturb him, Lorelei slipped out of his arms. Tucking the blanket around her sarong fashion, she moved to the mouth of the cave. It was still dark outside, but the rain had stopped some time ago. The moon glowed like a golden ball in the black sky. Stars shimmered like Christmas-tree lights painted on a midnight canvas. Her gaze swept over the horizon where the shadows of the Superstitions towered dark and foreboding like sinister demons waiting for unsuspecting prey. A chill raced down her spine, and Lorelei rubbed her arms at the eerie thought.

Turning around, she strangled the scream in her throat as she ran into Jack's naked chest. "Mercy, you nearly scared me half to death. I didn't hear you get up."

He closed his arms around her, stroked her back. "I woke up because I felt a part of me was missing. And I was right. You weren't beside me."

Her heart twisted a tiny bit, and she burrowed into the warm, hard muscles of his chest. "I couldn't sleep."

"I've got a perfect cure for insomnia."

Lorelei heard the smile in his voice. She lifted her head and gave him a reproving look. "You've got a one-track mind, Jack Storm."

"Only where you're concerned."

Lorelei's pulse jumped at the hungry look in his eyes. Her gaze dropped lower, skimming over the magnificent pair of wide shoulders, the muscled chest, the washboard belly with its trail of dark hair that streaked down to the fully aroused male. Her gaze shot back up to his face. Smiling, Jack reached for the edge of the blanket tucked between her breasts and pulled it free.

"This time," he whispered as he carried her and placed her in the center of the blanket that had served as their bed. "This time we go slow."

A breath shuddered through her as he feathered kisses over her cheeks, her jaw, the corner of her mouth. He parted her lips with his finger and tasted her.

Lorelei's head grew fuzzy. Her blood seemed to thicken in her veins as Jack made love to her with his mouth while his clever hands caressed her, shaped her, branded her with his touch.

His hand streaked lower, down her belly, to the curls that covered her womanhood. Slowly, oh so slowly, he eased his finger inside her and began to stroke the sensitized bud at her center. Over and over he continued the gentle torture. When the first spasm hit, Lorelei cried out as sensation rushed over her just as the rain had rushed down the mountainside. He repeated the movement again and again—first with his fingers, then with his mouth.

"Damn you, Jack," she sobbed as wave after wave of pleasure hit her. "I want you inside me."

He gazed up at her from between her legs. His hair was a wicked mess where she'd pulled it, speared it with her fingers. Dark stubble covered his jaw and chin, and his eyes were a sinful blue in that tanned face. "Not yet. I'm not finished pleasuring you yet."

She didn't know if she could take much more pleasure, Lorelei thought as he dipped his head again. She felt the brush of whiskers against her inner thighs and then at the mouth of her sex as he spread her open and tasted her again.

Minutes later, with her body still quivering, Lorelei grabbed his hair and dragged his mouth up to hers.

She could taste herself on his lips. The realization shocked her, excited her. She wanted to taste him. She rolled him over onto his back. Straddling him, she drew her tongue down his neck, his chest, and licked one flat nipple.

He shuddered and reached for her.

"No." She pushed him back to the makeshift bed and repeated the measure to his other nipple. She raked her teeth over the flat bud.

"W-where did you learn that?" he asked on a gasp.

She smiled up at him. "From you."

On the move again, she tasted and tormented him with her mouth, with her fingers as he had done her.

"Stop," he commanded as she closed her fist around him. "Oh, don't stop," he said, shuddering on the next breath as she licked the velvet tip of him with her tongue.

When she took him into her mouth, his eyes turned to smoke. "No more," he told her, and hauled her up his body. "I need to be inside you."

A surge of feminine power shot through her at his confession. He lifted her, guided her onto him, joining their bodies in the most elemental and timeless way—until she was no longer sure where her body ended or his began.

Then she began to move. Slowly she rocked back and forth, wanting to give him that same exquisite pleasure he had given her.

The fire began to build inside her again—hot and sweet and fast, filling her with its heat, filling her with a voracious need for more.

Jack palmed her breasts, squeezed them gently in his hands and set off another burst of flames inside her. She moved her body back and forth and felt the flames burn hot and fast, then hotter and faster still.

Just when she was sure she would explode, Jack clutched her hips, rolled her body beneath his and drove his shaft deeper. The first shudder hit her, stole her breath away, and before she could catch it again, he was easing his hand between them, stroking the sensitive bud of her womanhood even while he filled her with himself. When the next spasm hit her and sent her hurling into the fire, Jack was crying out her name and diving into the flames with her.

When Jack finally managed to lift his head again, the sun was just starting to come up. He glanced at the woman sleeping beside him. Fawn-colored curls shimmered like gold. White satin skin seemed to glow like pearls on the ugly green blanket.

Desire stirred in his belly again, and Jack marveled at his insatiable hunger for her. Would it ever not be like this between them? he wondered, and decided it wouldn't. As long as she was anywhere within ten feet of him, he would want her, feel the need to touch her. He wanted to touch her now, feel her body curl next to his. Feel her breasts press against his chest...

Jack kicked back the covers. If he lay here another minute looking at her, she wasn't going to get another moment's sleep. And she needed to sleep.

Taking care not to wake her, he slipped from the bed and retrieved his torn clothes from the rocks where Lorelei had left them to dry. After dressing, he massaged his shoulder, acknowledged the stiffness in his arm, then moved to the front of the cave.

Fingers of golden sunlight spilled onto the mountains in the east, making them glisten like polished gems. Water no longer rushed along the winding ridge outside of the cave, making it a dangerous and frightening path. The tumbled foothills of the canyons below resembled the gray green waves of a calm sea.

Jack thought of his backpack and the map he'd lost. Even if the pack had survived, he'd never find it now. He thought of Lorelei and the treasure of having her love him again and knew no gold mine, regardless of its riches, could ever compare with that.

But what kind of future could they possibly have now? The mine had been his hope for their future. How could he ask her to marry him now, to share her life with him, when he had nothing to offer her?

He couldn't, Jack decided. She deserved so much more. *If only...*

Frustrated, he bit off the thought. He'd do better to concentrate on getting them down the mountain instead of dwelling on what might have been. Again surveying the ridge that led to the canyon below, Jack paused as he spotted what appeared to be the remains of an old military trail.

He frowned as one of the Dutchman's riddles came back

to him. *From my mine you can see the military trail, but from the military trail you cannot see my mine.* Had he seen the cave from the trail below? He didn't think so. Hell, he hadn't even seen this ridge on the mountain, hadn't known it existed before yesterday.

My mine is located in a north-trending canyon. Jack stared around him; the cave was in a north-trending canyon. His heart picked up speed as he remembered one of the other clues he'd puzzled over.

There is a rock face on the trail to my mine. There was a rock face on the ridge leading to the cave that he had jumped to yesterday.

Excited, Jack stared at the area around him. *No miner will find my mine.* The riddles continued to pour from his memory. *The rays of the setting sun shine into the entrance of my mine.* But since he was facing east, the setting sun wouldn't shine on this ridge. Disappointed, Jack started to return to the cave. *There is a trick in the trail to my mine.* A trick? Jack frowned and rubbed at his jaw. A trick like a hidden cave? A cave with a secret entrance that faced west?

Jack felt the burning in his gut, the tingling at the back of the neck. The Dutchman's Mine. Somewhere in or around the cave was the Lost Dutchman's Gold Mine. And if he could find it, then he wouldn't have to give Lorelei up. Adrenaline spiking through him, Jack rushed back along the path to the cave.

Lorelei looked up from where she had spread out their remaining rations on the blanket. "What is it? What's wrong?"

"I think I know where the Dutchman's Mine is." Jack swooped down to kiss her shocked mouth.

"Where?"

"I'm not sure exactly, but somewhere in or around this cave."

"But how?" she asked as she slowly came to her feet.

"You lost the map with your backpack. I saw it go down into the canyon myself."

"I know. I know," he replied, barely able to keep still he was so excited. "It's the riddles. The Dutchman's riddles. They point to this place."

Quickly Jack went through the scenario. Taking her outside, he pointed to the trail and the northern trend of the canyon, and brought her back to the front of the cave.

"Jack, it's still a long shot. Maybe we should go back to the camp and come back later once we've gotten some supplies."

"We don't have time, Lorelei. I'm not even sure we could find this spot again. Don't worry, the rain's over and I promise we'll leave long before nightfall. But first let's look for the mine." He paused and looked into her eyes. "I love you. I want us to have a life together, but without the treasure or at least a part of it, I have nothing to offer you."

"I don't want anything but you."

"I want to marry you, have children with you. But I need to be able to come to you with something more than my love and a promise."

"Your love is all I want. I have a job, Jack."

"No. I'm not going to live off of you." He paused and confessed his plans. "There's a boat company back in Florida where I've been working on and off for the past five years. I like the work," he admitted. "And I'm pretty good at it. I have a chance to buy the place. But to do that, I need money. If I were to find the mine, I'd be able to buy it and then I could ask you to marry me."

"You don't need the mine, Jack. I've got some money saved. You can have it. If it's not enough, we can borrow the rest."

He kissed her fingertips. "I appreciate the offer, but I couldn't take money from you. No. I need to do this on my own. If I find the mine, I can buy the company and then you and I can get married."

"And if you don't find the mine? What happens then? Will we still get married?"

"We'd have to wait."

He watched the sparkle in her eyes dissolve. "How long?"

"As long as it takes. Please try to understand, I can't come to you with nothing a second time—not if I want to keep my self-respect."

"I feel like we're right back to where we started ten years ago. You didn't show up to marry me because you went off on some dive to look for treasure because you wanted a bigger start for us, and look what happened then."

"This is different. History isn't going to repeat itself. This time you're with me. We're going to find that mine and once we do, I'll buy the boat company and we'll get married just like we planned. Before you know it, we'll be busy working on having a family."

"Are you sure, Jack? Are you really sure that's what you want? I don't want to lose you again."

"You're not going to lose me. Trust me, sweetheart. The mine is here, and we're going to find it. I can feel it in my gut."

"And your gut is never wrong," she concluded. She let out a long sigh. "All right. Where do you want me to start?"

"That's my girl." He gave her another swift kiss. "You start out here in front of the cave, and I'll look for another way inside from the back."

Lorelei hesitated. "You really believe the mine's here?"

"I can feel it in my bones."

Four hours later Lorelei stretched and wiped her face with the tail of her shirt. The only thing she was feeling in her bones at the moment was weariness. If the mine was here, it was keeping itself well hidden. Hot and thirsty, she dusted off her hands and moved inside of the cave to retrieve her canteen.

After taking a long drink, she refastened the top and bent over to search her backpack for a ponytail tie. As she leaned over, she caught a glint of something shiny on the floor at the far end of the cave.

Lorelei hesitated. Once she'd gotten Jack into the cave yesterday, she hadn't had much chance to explore their surroundings. As far as she could tell, the small cave was just that—a hollowed-out cavern the size of a room. Others had used it. She'd determined that by the dried-out sticks in one corner and the remnants of a long-ago fire. She'd done her best to ignore the pieces of what appeared to be a skeleton that lurked in the narrow and darkest curve at the end of the cave.

She took another step closer and caught the glint of something gold again. The Dutchman's Mine? A shiver of excitement raced through her as she edged farther toward the cave's end. She saw what looked like the remains of a skull, and an icy chill zipped down her spine. Suddenly she remembered the tales about people disappearing who'd come in search of the mine. Maybe it was the gold tooth of some old prospector who had died here.

She shuddered at the unpleasant thought, but moved a little closer. Then she remembered the Indian tales of spirits haunting the mountains. Some of the old-timers who lived in the area claimed it was the Dutchman himself protecting his mine from claim jumpers.

"Don't be ridiculous," Lorelei muttered to herself, feeling like a ninny for letting her imagination run wild. She nudged the skull with her boot, and her heart jumped to her throat as something slithered beneath the rock.

Removing the flashlight she'd hooked to her belt, she shone it on the rock and up the wall. She touched the wall and found it damp. Angling the light again, she searched out the spot where she thought she'd seen that glint of gold. There just to the left of another cluster of rocks, it flashed again. Stooping down, she picked up a small chunk of gold no bigger than the size of a quarter.

"Oh, my God," she whispered. Closing her trembling fingers around the nugget, she ran from the cave screaming for Jack.

Jack caught her as she exited the cave at a dead run. Eyes wide with fear, he grabbed her by the arms. "What is it? Did something happen? Are you hurt?"

Laughter bubbled out of her. She felt happy. Excited. Scared to death.

"For God sakes, Lorelei." He gave her a little shake. "Tell me what's wrong."

"This," she said, still barely able to speak. She held up the chunk of gold.

"What?" he said, looking at her as though he thought she'd lost her mind.

"This," she told him again, waving the piece of gold in front of his nose. "It's a gold nugget."

"A gold nugget," he repeated. "You mean—"

She dissolved into laughter again and wrapped her arms around him. "Oh Jack, I think I've found the Lost Dutchman's Gold Mine."

Eleven

"You were right," Jack told her. Using the small pickax that had somehow managed to remain hooked to his belt during the storm, he pried away the rotting board hidden by the cluster of rocks.

Dust sprayed him as the wood splintered to reveal a small tunnel. Coughing, Jack made Lorelei stay back as he tore away another board. "Okay," he said. "Shine the light inside."

Lorelei gasped. "It's gold."

"Yes," Jack acknowledged as he caught the shimmer along the walls. Gold winked at him—chunks the size of a man's fist just waiting to be dug out of the rock. They had found the Lost Dutchman's Mine. It was the culmination of a lifetime of quests for him, every treasure hunter's dream to make a find of this size. And he owed it all to Lorelei. After all his years of searching for the mother lode, it had taken Lorelei to lead him to it.

A smile spread across his face and in his heart. He turned

to her, cupped her beautiful face with his dirty hands. "You know what this means, don't you?"

"Yes," she said, laughing. "It means now you have no excuse not to marry me."

He kissed her long and hard with the joy and excitement of the find, with the joy and excitement of the future that awaited them. Reluctantly he set her away.

"All right. What do we do next?" she asked.

"*You* just stand over there, shine the light for me and look beautiful while I gouge out a stake for our future."

She frowned. "But I want to help."

"Sweetheart, the best way to help me is to stay out of the way. This tunnel looks like it's ready to give any minute." And that nagging in his gut told him it was liable to happen sooner than he'd like. "If you insist on coming inside with me, I'll be too worried about you to get the job done."

"But, Jack, you'll never be able to get the gold out of those walls by yourself."

"I'm not greedy. I'm not looking to clean the place out. I just want enough to be able to buy that boat place and give us a start. Besides, even if I could get the mountain to give up its gold, I wouldn't be able to haul it down without the proper equipment. I won't be long. I promise. Here." He removed the pouch with the rings from his pocket and handed them to her. "You just sit there and think about what kind of wedding you want."

He paused and kissed her again. "Just make sure whatever you decide on that it takes place within the week. I've waited ten years to make you my wife. I don't intend to wait a second longer than I have to once we get back off this mountain."

Turning from her, Jack went inside the tunnel and started to work. He chiseled, he picked away at the walls, trying to go slowly so as not to upset the already shaky structure. He wiped sweat and dust from his face and eyes.

After several hours his muscles ached and the pain in his shoulder screamed for him to stop, but he continued, determined to chip away enough of the gold to give him that new start he wanted. A new life with Lorelei as his wife. The shell of the mine rumbled and shook in protest, sending more dirt spraying down on his head. Each time it did so, the vibrations lasted longer.

"Jack, are you all right?"

He whipped his head around at the sound of Loreli so close. His heart almost stopped as he saw the light balanced on a rock and Loreli stooping down not more that five feet away picking up small pieces of gold. "Lorelei!"

She rose to her feet and started to hold out her hand. "I was just—"

"Get out of here," he commanded. "I told you it's not safe in here."

When she opened her mouth to argue, he held up his hand. "Please, sweetheart," he said, his voice sounding as weary as he felt, "wait for me outside the tunnel. I won't be much longer. All I need is a couple more chunks and then we can go."

She hesitated a moment, then tucking her hand in her pocket, moved back out of the tunnel.

An hour later Jack dug free another chunk of gold and rock and added it to the small cache. Wrapping them in the shirt he'd taken off and fashioned for carrying, he began making his way back to the front of the tunnel.

Lorelei screamed, and in his haste to get to her, he tripped over a rock and sent the gold and rocks scattering around him. Dust shook from the trembling timbers. When Lorelei cried out again, Jack hurried to his feet and raced out to the cave, leaving the gold behind.

The blood froze in his veins at the sight of her lying on the floor at the tunnel's entrance, clutching her right hand with her left and writhing in pain.

In a heartbeat he was beside her. "What happened? What's wrong?" he asked, rushing to her side.

"S-spider bite," she managed to say between lips clenched tight and turning white with pain. "Tarantula, I think. It bit me when I tried to move the rock."

A tarantula. Jack paled. Although it wasn't deadly, the bite could be extremely painful. "Let me see," he told her as he pried her fingers away from her hand. The area was red and already swelling. "I know it hurts, baby."

He kissed the reddening skin and carried her to the blanket they'd shared the previous night. "I'm going to give you a couple of aspirin. It's not much, but it might take the edge off the pain for now," he explained. Ignoring the sound of rumbling and creaking timbers coming from the tunnel, Jack focused on Lorelei. "Open your mouth for me, sweetheart." He placed the pills on her tongue and brought the canteen to her lips.

"Jack," she gasped. Her body shook in his arms, and she clutched at her throat. "N-need to get to hospital. H-having allergic reaction."

His heart missed a beat. His pulse came to a stop. "You're allergic to spiders?"

She nodded. "M-must be. I...I had same reaction to b-bee and wasp stings," she told him as another shiver racked her body. She clutched at her throat again and seemed to fight for breath. "N-need to g-get to the hospital. Th-throat. W-will die if throat c-closes up."

And the hospital was at the bottom of the mountain. "You're not going to die. I won't let you die. Don't worry. I'll get you to the hospital."

He wasn't sure she heard him; she seemed to drift off. Hooking the canteen to his belt, he strapped the pack to his back and lifted Lorelei into his arms. He carried her out into the sunlight. Her face was the color of chalk, and a sheen of cold sweat beaded her brow.

Jack started down the ridge. Heedless of the sun burning

his face and back, the suffocating heat that made breathing hurt, he focused on the trail that would lead him to the camp.

"Lorelei, can you hear me?"

She seemed to be drifting in and out of consciousness. Jack vacillated between fear that her condition was deteriorating and gratitude that she could escape the pain at least for a little while.

"Th-thirsty," she told him.

Jack eased her body to rest against a boulder and unscrewed the cap of the canteen. He allowed her to drink her fill. His own mouth was dry, but he didn't drink, wanting there to be enough if she needed more. He recapped the canteen and rehooked it to his belt without taking a drink.

"D-did you get the gold?" she asked him as he lifted her again and started down the mountain once more.

"No."

"But the mine. You said we couldn't find it again without the map."

"Don't worry about the mine," he told her. "I don't care about the gold. All that matters to me is getting you to the hospital."

What good were a hundred gold mines if she were to die? Lorelei had been right, Jack thought as he continued down the mountain, hating himself for endangering her as he had. She'd accused him once of not growing up, of risking his life looking for treasures. And she'd been right.

He'd opted for a life of failed get-rich-quick schemes instead of working hard and making something of himself. Even when the fates had offered him another chance with Lorelei, he'd foolishly failed to snatch it. No, not him. Not Jack Storm. Just one more quest. One more try for the quick fix.

And look what it had cost him.

"Hurts." Lorelei squirmed in his arms. "Everything hurts," she whimpered.

Jack swallowed and fought back the urge to weep. "Hang on, sweetheart. Hang on just a little longer. I'll have you there soon."

Dear God, he prayed as he forged his way down the canyon. *Please let her live. If you let her live, I'll get out of her life for good.*

She grew steadily paler as the hours ticked by. When she had him stop so she could be sick, Jack wept. Tears ran down his dirty cheeks as he mopped her brow and gave her another dose of aspirin for the pain. Then he picked her up and was on the move again.

By the time he reached the edge of the canyon that led to their campsite, the sun was dipping in the sky. Lorelei's face was nearly gray. Her hair was damp, and her skin was fevered. He'd long ago stopped feeling the ache in his arms, the cramp in his legs.

Forcing himself, he covered the remaining distance to the campsite. His stomach sank. The tent was gone; only pieces of the frame remained. The Coleman stove lay smashed against a rock.

Jack began to climb the ridge to the road where he'd parked the Explorer. If the truck was gone, he'd never make it back to civilization in time.

He nearly dropped to his knees in thanksgiving when he saw it still sitting there unharmed. Moving to the front of the vehicle, he leaned Lorelei against the hood and reached under the front bumper catch to fish out the spare key he'd secured there for emergencies.

After placing Lorelei into the passenger seat and strapping her in, Jack started the truck and headed out onto the darkening stretch of road and raced toward Apache Junction.

When he pulled the Explorer to a stop at the hospital's

emergency entrance, Jack ignored the security guard who insisted he had to move the vehicle.

He shoved open the doors with his boot and carried Lorelei inside. "I need a doctor," Jack told the wide-eyed woman behind the admittance desk. "Now," he said in a harsh voice when she continued to stare.

The woman raced from the room and returned with a kid in a white doctor's coat. The guy barely looked old enough to shave. "You a doctor?" Jack asked skeptically.

"That's what they tell me. What's the problem?" he asked.

"She was bit by a spider. Tarantula."

The other man grimaced. "Nasty bite."

"It's more than nasty, it's deadly. She's allergic."

The man was all speed after that. "Put her on the gurney," he instructed Jack as he led him into the hospital emergency room that had been sectioned into cubicles. He put the stethoscope to Lorelei's chest, checked her pulse. He pulled the tips of the instrument from his ears. "Her blood pressure's too low. And she's in shock." He lifted the lids of her eyes.

She was so pale, her lips almost blue. For a moment Jack thought he was going to be ill.

"What's your name?"

"Jack. Jack Storm."

"This your wife, Jack?" he asked as he continued to examine Lorelei.

Jack swallowed, felt that bitter ache in his chest. "No. My fiancée." Or at least she had been. He'd made his bargain with the Almighty and would keep it. If Lorelei was allowed to pull through this, he would do the only unselfish and responsible thing he'd ever done in his life. He'd walk away from her.

"What's your fiancée's name?"

"Lorelei. Her name's Lorelei Mason."

"Pretty name for a pretty lady."

Jack had to give it to the kid doctor. When it came to bedside manner, he was good. He kept the conversation calm and even while he continued to check her vital signs.

He opened Lorelei's mouth, probed inside with a tongue depressor. Her tongue was thick and swollen. "Her esophagus is swollen, and her breathing's shallow." He turned to the nurse waiting beside him. "Get me five cc's of epinephrine stat."

Within seconds the nurse was handing him a syringe. Jack winced as he injected something into Lorelei's arm. He felt helpless as he watched the doctor and nurse work on her. Worse, he felt guilty. He knew it was his fault that Lorelei was lying there. Had he not been so selfish, she would be safely married to Van Owen by now and not fighting for her life.

"Get a unit of calcium gluconate started," he ordered the nurse. "How long ago did she get bit?" the doctor asked as he continued to monitor her vital signs.

"I don't know. Six, maybe seven hours."

"Where?"

"Up in the Superstitions." He gave him the general vicinity that they'd been in.

"Where's the bite?"

Jack showed him the red swollen patch near her wrist.

"Do you know if she's allergic to any drugs?" His voice was calm, but his hands continued to move quickly. A new bag was hung on the IV stand and fed into the vein in Lorelei's arm. The doctor thumped the tube with his finger.

"I don't know. Maybe her parents or one of her sisters can tell you. I could call them." It would have to be collect since his wallet had been lost with his backpack.

"Why don't you do that. You're also going to need to give the admit clerk some information on Ms. Mason."

"Doc, is she going to be all right?"

"Let's hope so, Jack. Let's hope so. I don't know how you got her down that mountain and in here so fast. My guess is you carried her most of the way. But I can tell you however you did it, you probably saved her life. Another hour and...''

Jack knew what the doctor didn't say. Lorelei could've died. And it would have been his fault. ''Is she going to make it?'' Jack demanded.

''If she responds to the drugs, she will. You've done everything you can. Why don't you go call her parents, maybe get yourself a shower and change of clothes.''

Jack looked down at the shirt he'd found in the truck and thrown on without bothering to button. His jeans were ragged. His body was covered with streaks of red dirt. His eyes still gritty from sweat and dust, and he hadn't seen a razor in days. He probably looked like a madman to everyone here.

He didn't care. ''I'll call her family and use the hospital bathroom. But I'm not leaving here until I know she's all right.''

A few minutes later in the men's room, Jack splashed his face with water and tried to wash off some of the mountain's grime from his skin. The call to Lorelei's mother hadn't been an easy one to make. The woman had been far easier on him than he'd deserved.

Leaning over the basin, he stared at his face in the mirror. His eyes were shadowed and dull. With the dark stubble covering his jaw and chin and his hair still damp from the dunking under the faucet, he looked every inch the pirate Lorelei had once called him.

And like the marauding pirate he was, he'd nearly destroyed something good and precious. God willing, he would try to put it back together again.

Lorelei opened her eyes and blinked at the people standing at the end of her bed. ''Mom? Dad?''

''Oh, thank God.'' Her mother rushed to her side. Hands

fluttering, eyes misting, she stroked Lorelei's cheek. "Oh, my poor baby. How do you feel?"

"Thirsty," she said, struggling to sit up to drink from the glass that her father was handing her. The water was cool and soothing as it slid down her throat. "Thanks," she said, and lay back down. Her body felt as if it had been through a marathon workout session.

"Where am I?"

"In the hospital in Apache Junction," her father answered.

"The hospital," she repeated, surveying the standard-issue white walls, the ascetic-looking drapes, the tubes running in her arm.

"You were bit by a spider, and Jack had to carry you down the mountain...."

She barely heard her mother's chatter as the events began to come back to her in bits and pieces. The flash flood. She and Jack making love. Discovering the gold mine. The spider biting her on the hand. She remembered the sound of the tunnel starting to crumble and Jack's shattered expression as he'd carried her outside the cave to safety. Why wasn't Jack here with her? "Where's Jack?" she asked, suddenly frightened.

"Waiting outside," her mother told her.

"The boy should be horsewhipped for carting you off like he did from the church," her father said, puffing up very Spencer Tracy-like, reminding Lorelei how often he allowed his resemblance to the late actor to spill over into his mannerisms. "I'd have taken a whip to him, too, if he hadn't looked like he was about ready to take the whip to himself."

Lorelei's heart twisted. Of course, the stupid man was probably out there blaming himself. "Daddy," she interrupted her father as he went into another Spencer Tracy-like speech. "I need to see him. I need to talk to Jack."

"I don't know, baby doll. You've just come through a nasty time, and both of your sisters are waiting to see you."

"Daddy, I *need* to see Jack."

"Let me check with the doctor first—"

"Daddy, either you bring Jack in here or I'll get up and go find him myself."

Her father blinked and gave her a stern look. "And since when do you speak to me in that tone, young lady? I might have expected this from one of your sisters. Desiree with her causes and Clea with her women's lib, but not from you. You were always such a good, sensible girl."

"Oh, Henry, for pity's sake. Put a sock in it and go get the boy for her."

"Thanks, Mom," Lorelei said as her father made a regal exit.

"It's all right, dear. Sometimes your father just gets caught up in the moment. He's working on the remake of an old Spencer Tracy film. It's only as one of the extras, a guest at a wedding, but I'm afraid the Tracy influence from the original film has spilled over and into his head."

Lorelei couldn't help but laugh. Her parents were a wonder. After spending a lifetime chasing their dream of making it in the movies, the two of them were as much in love with one another now as they had been as teenagers. It was the kind of love that endured. The kind of love and life she wanted with Jack.

Her mother smoothed Lorelei's hair back from her face. "You're in love with him, aren't you?"

"Yes. I love him with all my heart. I think I always have, even when I thought I hated him."

Her mother smiled. "Love happens that way sometimes. Though he often drives me crazy and I swear I'll murder him someday, the truth is, I can't imagine my life without your father. I know I wouldn't want to go through this life without him beside me."

"That's how I feel about Jack. I don't want to spend another minute of my life without him to share it with."

"Then I think you've got your work cut out for you, dear. He's carrying an awful lot of guilt around inside him over what happened to you on that mountain."

"But it wasn't his fault the spider bit me. He saved my life by getting me to the hospital."

"And that's what you're going to have to convince him of. If you truly love him, Lorelei, fight for him."

Lorelei marveled at the woman who had given birth to her. Even at fifty-two, her mother was still a remarkably beautiful woman with her auburn hair and hazel eyes. And in addition to being beautiful, she was smart.

But before she could tell her so, Jack was walking through the door. He looked tired, beaten, like a man condemned to the gallows. His handsome face was somber, and there was no trace of that reckless smile she loved. But it was his eyes; they made her heart ache. They were still the same sinful shade of blue, but gone was the spark of mischief, the hint of laughter. They looked flat, dull, dead.

"Hi, beautiful. How are you feeling?" he asked, making no move to come closer.

"Better. Almost like new."

"I think I'll go let the doctor and your sisters know that you're awake," her mother offered. Mouthing "Good luck," she slipped out of the room.

"You look a lot better than you did last night," he informed her.

"Too bad I can't say the same for you. When's the last time you slept, Jack?"

He shrugged. "I got a few winks on the waiting-room couch last night."

"And if I know you, you spent most of it beating yourself up over what happened to me."

"That's not true," he started to argue, but abandoned the lie when she arched her brow. "All right. What if I did? I certainly had enough reason to. I nearly got you killed over some damn gold mine."

"Would you please quit hovering at the door like you're ready to bolt and come here."

"And how are you feeling, Ms. Mason?" A young doctor with the name Stevens embroidered across his pocket came into the room. "You gave us all quite a scare last night, young lady. Especially Jack. The nurses are still talking about the half-naked mountain man who carried you in here demanding you be treated."

Before she could respond, he plunked a thermometer in her mouth and lifted her wrist to take her pulse. When he removed the thermometer, he made a notation on her chart and then chucked the disposable part into the trash. He told her to open her mouth.

"Ah, better. Much better. I think we can dispense with the IV."

"When can I leave?" Lorelei finally managed to get a word in.

"If your vitals remain steady, I think we can discharge you sometime tomorrow. I'll let your sisters know they can come in to see you now." He clamped a hand on Jack's shoulder. "Keep an eye on our patient, Jack. And don't let her overtire herself."

"I'll do that."

Her two sisters burst in the room. "Oh, Lorelei, will you ever forgive me?" Desiree, ever the actress, was weeping and carrying on like the heroine in a Southern novel.

"Will you stop with the waterworks, Desiree," Clea demanded. She scowled at Jack and then turned to Lorelei. "Do you want me to toss him out for you?"

From the serious expression on her sister's face and knowing how little use her older sister had for the male population in general, Lorelei said, "No, thanks. I've decided to keep him."

Clea frowned. "What about Herbert?"

"You know he and his mother took off for Europe to get away from the scandal," Desiree explained.

"The scandal?" Lorelei repeated.

"Mm-hmm. Of Herbert being left standing at the altar," Clea said, a smile tugging at her lips.

"And it's all my fault," Desiree said with a sniffle.

"Clea, Desiree. I need to speak with Jack. Alone."

Clea shifted her gaze from Lorelei to Jack and back again. "You sure that's what you want?"

"I'm sure," she told her. Jack was all she would ever want.

"All right. Come on, brat." She hooked her arm through the weeping Desiree's. "Let's go pretty up that ugly face of yours. I heard that handsome Dr. Stevens was asking mother about you."

"He was?" Desiree said as the two of them left the hospital room.

"Jack—"

"Lorelei—"

"You first," Lorelei told him.

"I want to apologize. I know it's a little late and saying I'm sorry won't make up for all the pain I've caused you. And Lord knows I've caused you enough pain to last two lifetimes." He paced from one end of her bed to the other.

"Exactly what is it you're apologizing for, Jack?"

"Everything."

"Everything?"

"Yes."

"Does that include telling me you love me? Making love to me?"

"No." He stilled and drove his fingers through his hair. "I'm not sorry for that. I can't be. You're the best thing that's ever happened to me."

She caught his hand as he made another pass by her. She looked into his eyes, wanting to take away all that pain and guilt she saw there. "And you're the best thing that's happened to me, Jack. The very best."

"How can you say that?"

"Easily. I love you."

He started to pull away, but she refused to let go of him. "I'm not going to let you walk out on me, Jack. You said if we found the mine, you would marry me. Well, I found the mine. And even if it is my fault you lost the gold—"

"I don't give a damn about the gold or the mine. I almost got you killed."

"You saved my life."

Jack snorted. "Yeah, after almost causing you to lose it."

"I'm not letting you off the hook, Jack Storm. You're going to marry me."

He looked at her as though she'd lost her mind. "You're crazy. Do you know that? How can you still want to marry me? All I've done is cause you pain. I let you down ten years ago. I wasn't even there when you lost. . ." He swallowed and started again. "When you lost our baby. I even ruined your chance to marry a good man, a man who's made something of his life. A man with a lot more to offer you than some foolhardy dreams."

He shook his head. "I almost cost you your life. I won't let you throw it away now because of me. I love you too much. I'm going to talk to Van Owen, square things with him for you. I'll explain that this whole thing was my fault, that you didn't want to go with me. Then you and he can patch things up."

That had cost him. She could see it in his eyes. She took hope from that. "I don't want to patch things up with Herbert. At least not the way you mean."

"Sure, you do. I'll talk to him for you. Now, you get some rest and I'll come back to see you before you're discharged."

"Coward," Lorelei called after him as he rushed out the door.

Jack slipped out of the hospital room and leaned against the door. He had to let her go. It was the right thing to do. He owed her that much. And the best place to start would be by squaring things with Herbert as he'd promised her.

By the time Jack reached Herbert Van Owen III in Paris and had the other man call Lorelei back at the hospital, he felt as though he'd cut off his right arm. And he was already finding it difficult to live with his decision. He didn't want to let Lorelei go.

He'd done the right thing, Jack reminded himself as he walked down the corridor of the hospital the next morning.

"Ah, Jack," Dr. Stevens called to him. "I'm getting ready to release your fiancée."

"That's great, Doc."

"Give me five minutes and you can collect your future bride and get on with those wedding plans." He gave Jack a wink. "I hear your lady's decided not to waste any time. Her mother tells me the wedding's set for this weekend."

Jack nearly choked. So much for having to worry about Herbert not understanding. And Lorelei certainly hadn't wasted any time putting things right back on track between her and Herbert.

Not that he blamed her, Jack told himself, biting back the bitter taste in his mouth as he thought of her and Van Owen. He headed for her room to say his goodbyes.

Taking a deep breath, Jack pushed open the door. His chest ached at the sight of Lorelei smiling and chatting with the doctor. "Now don't forget, I want you to come to the wedding. This Saturday at ten o'clock."

"I'll be there," Dr. Stevens told her. After giving her the last of her instructions, he departed the room.

"I was wondering if you were going to come back."

"I said I would," he said, unable to keep the edge out of his voice.

"It was sweet of you to call Herbert." She brushed her fawn-colored curls and tucked the brush in the overnight bag her mother had brought to the hospital.

"Looks like you two patched things up after all."

"Looks like it." She snapped the case closed and turned to face him. She gave him that siren smile that made his knees weak. "I guess you've heard I'm getting married on Saturday."

"Yeah, I heard." Jealousy clawed at his gut. "Looks like you decided not to waste any time, either."

"Can you blame me? I've planned to marry twice now, and neither wedding has come off. I thought the best thing would be to do it as quickly as possible before the groom changes his mind."

She picked up the case and walked to the closet and removed the shirt and slacks she'd been wearing when he'd brought her into the hospital.

"You never said, were you planning on searching for the Dutchman's Mine again?" she asked while folding the shirt in smooth lines. She placed it inside the bag.

"I haven't decided." How could he even think of searching for the mine again? The thought of looking for it and even finding the treasure again held no appeal for him—not when he'd lost the only treasure that he wanted. Not when he'd lost her.

"I can't believe you're not going to go back and try to find the mine again."

"Treasure hunting's lost some of its appeal." Right now all he wanted to do was grab her by the shoulders, kiss her senseless and tell her he wouldn't let her marry anyone but him.

"But what about that company in Florida? I thought you needed to find the mine so you'd have the money to buy it."

He shrugged. "Maybe I'll be able to work something out with the owner and the bank when I get back."

"When is that?"

"When is what?"

"When will you be going back to Florida?"

He shoved his hand through his hair. "I don't know. In a few days probably."

"Then you'll still be here for the weekend?"

"Yeah. I'll probably be here." And if she invited him to her wedding, he *would* strangle her.

"How much money would it take for you to make a down payment on that boat company you wanted?" she asked as she added her boots to the bag.

"Probably twice as much as I've got. I don't know. Why?"

She dug into the pocket of the slacks she'd stored in the bag and withdrew a handful of nuggets. Smiling, she walked over to Jack and offered them to him. "Would this help any? It's what I picked up in the mine."

Dumbfounded, angry, Jack stared at the gold and at her. "I don't want your damn gold. You think you have to pay me off to make sure I don't ruin your wedding plans on Saturday? Do you really think I could actually stick around here and watch you marry some other guy? Keep your gold, Lorelei. I don't intend to be anywhere near this place come Saturday."

"Jack, wait," she called out to him as he turned and started for the door.

He didn't stop. If he did, he knew he wouldn't be able to leave. He'd break all of his vows and good intentions by falling at her feet and begging her for another chance.

"Jack!" She caught his arm as he reached for the door.

"What?" He refused to look at her, couldn't look at her.

She cupped his cheek with her fingers and forced him to look at her. "I'm going to have a real problem if you leave before Saturday. And I'm afraid my parents, especially my father, will be really upset with you if you do leave."

Jack frowned as he tried to make sense of what she was saying. "Why?"

She pulled the pouch with the wedding rings from her pocket. "Because you're the groom I'm planning to marry on Saturday. I love you, Jack Storm. Only you. And I want to spend the rest of my life with you."

"I need to sit down," he told her, and did so right there on the floor. "What about Van Owen? I thought... He's everything you always wanted. He's dependable, responsible. He's got a good job, security."

She dropped down beside him. "And I'd be bored silly. Maybe that's what I thought I wanted or told myself I wanted when I lost you all those years ago. But you were right when you said I was still an adventuress at heart. I am. The only security I need is knowing you love me."

"Lorelei, I wasn't lying when I told you I don't have anything to offer you. I don't even know if any bank will be willing to lend me the money to buy that boat outfit in Florida."

"Then we'll find another bank that will. Better yet," she continued, "why don't we go find us another gold mine and buy the place outright?"

"You're crazy, do you know that?"

"Crazy in love with you."

"What about the home you wanted? The security that was so important to you?"

"The only home I need is you, Jack. Wherever you are is the only home I'll ever want or need. I love you."

"Come on," Jack told her as he pulled them both to their feet and scooped her up into his arms.

Laughing, Lorelei asked, "Where are we going?"

Jack kissed her with all the love and hope in his heart. Then he smiled, curving his lips into what she'd always called his pirate's smile. "You're being kidnapped, sweetheart."

"Again."

"Yes."

"Where to this time?

"To find the nearest minister."

* * * * *

Look for SWITCHED AT THE ALTAR,
the next book of Metsy Hingle's
RIGHT BRIDE, WRONG GROOM *series,*
coming to you in March 1998,
and BODYGUARD AND THE BRIDESMAID,
coming in May 1998 from Silhouette Desire.

Desire Crystal Sweepstakes
Official Rules—No Purchase Necessary

To enter, complete an Official Entry Form or 3" x 5" card by hand printing the words "Desire Crystal Sweepstakes," your name and address thereon and mailing it to: in the U.S., Desire Crystal Sweepstakes, P.O. Box 9076, Buffalo, NY 14269-9076; in Canada, Desire Crystal Sweepstakes, P.O. Box 637, Fort Erie, Ontario L2A 5X3. Limit: one entry per envelope, one prize to an individual, family or organization. Entries must be sent via first-class mail and be received no later than 12/31/97. No responsibility is assumed for lost, late, misdirected or nondelivered mail.

Winners will be selected in random drawings (to be conducted no later than 1/31/98) from among all eligible entries received by D. L. Blair, Inc., an independent judging organization whose decisions are final. The prizes and their approximate values are: Grand Prize—a Mikasa Crystal Vase ($140 U.S.); 4 Second Prizes—a set of 4 Mikasa Crystal Champagne Flutes ($50 U.S. each set).

Sweepstakes offer is open only to residents of the U.S. (except Puerto Rico) and Canada who are 18 years of age or older, except employees and immediate family members of Harlequin Enterprises, Ltd., their affiliates, subsidiaries and all other agencies, entities and persons connected with the use, marketing or conduct of this sweepstakes. All applicable laws and regulations apply. Offer void wherever prohibited by law. Taxes and/or duties on prizes are the sole responsibility of the winners. Any litigation within the province of Quebec respecting the conduct and awarding of a prize in this sweepstakes may be submitted to the Régie des alcools, des courses et des jeux. All prizes will be awarded; winners will be notified by mail. No substitution for prizes is permitted. Odds of winning are dependent upon the number of eligible entries received.

Any prize or prize notification returned as undeliverable may result in the awarding of that prize to an alternative winner. By acceptance of their prize, winners consent to use of their names, photographs or likenesses for purposes of advertising, trade and promotion on behalf of Harlequin Enterprises, Ltd., without further compensation unless prohibited by law. In order to win a prize, residents of Canada will be required to correctly answer a time-limited, arithmetical skill-testing question administered by mail.

For a list of winners (available after January 31, 1998), send a separate stamped, self-addressed envelope to: Desire Crystal Sweepstakes 5309 Winners, P.O. Box 4200, Blair, NE 68009-4200, U.S.A.

Sweepstakes sponsored by Harlequin Enterprises Ltd., P.O. Box 9042, Buffalo, NY 14269-9042.

15YRRULE